Plenty of Harm in God

Plenty of Harm in God

a novel

Dana Bath

New Writers Series edited by Robert Allen

Design by conundrum press

Cover photo of church door and author photo by Andy Brown
Photos of Ireland by Corey Frost
An excerpt of this novel first appeared in *Matrix #54*

National Library of Canada Cataloguing in Publication Data

Bath, Dana, 1970-
    Plenty of harm in God

ISBN 0-919688-80-2 (bound) - ISBN 0-919688-78-0 (pbk.)

    I. Title.

PS8553.A829P64 2001   C813'.6   C2001-900982-8
PR9199.4.B38P64 2001

DC Books gratefully acknowledges the support of The Canada
Council for the Arts and of SODEC for our publishing program.

DC BOOKS / LIVRES DC
C.P. 662, 950 rue Decarie
Montreal, Quebec
H4L 4V9, Canada

The Canada Council | Le Conseil des Arts
for the Arts | du Canada

Acknowledgements

I would like to thank Robert Allen for his invaluable advice in developing the final manuscript of *Plenty of Harm in God*.

For reading earlier drafts and excerpts and providing me with constructive and inspirational feedback, I would like to thank: Taien Ng-Chan, Liane Keightley and Maria Francesca LoDico; Corey Frost; Erin Vollick and Meg Sircom; my thesis readers, Judith Herz and Mary di Michele; Catherine Bush and the members of her 1998-99 Concordia University Graduate Prose Workshop; and Michael Heffernan, Mickey Gorman, Mike McCormack and the participants in the 1999 University of Arkansas Summer Writer's Program in Galway, Ireland.

one

Molly

I

My father, your grandfather, was a very rich man.

When I was nine he placed me in a boarding school in St. John's. It was a charity school with an orphanage attached; rich parents felt that sending their children there was an act of kindness, as they were paying for the education of orphans at the same time. But St. Margaret's, my father said, had a very good reputation.

My sister Rosary had been at St. Margaret's since she was nine too. She planned to teach there one day, and the school was happy about her plan, because she was such a strong, intelligent, sensible girl.

I expected, in an institution full of nuns, to leave more of an impression than Rosary did, because I was divinely blessed. My father had said so since I was a baby. My mother was old when I was conceived; the doctors had told her she couldn't have any more children. My father said that at the moment I was born, he was sitting on the steps of the Grace Hospital and saw a cloud of doves rising out of a birch tree. There are no doves in Newfoundland as far as I know, so I agree it was quite a miracle. My father said that when I was baptized I didn't cry; I sang *"Be Thou My Vision"* in baby syllables. My mother always laughed at this story; she claimed I was saying the things all babies say.

My father said that when I was three years old, he brought me to the Basilica for the first time since my baptism, on a cloudy day, and I stepped into the church before him and light burst through the stained-glass windows in rainbow streams, and I genuflected without being taught how, and the whole building shook suddenly, "with the portent of God," he said. My mother agreed there was a tremor on that day, but she wasn't at the church, and she refused to believe the sunbeam-and-genuflexion story.

Is it surprising that I expected a school full of nuns to notice? But I think nuns are more skeptical now than people were in Biblical times, less open to miracles. The only hint that they saw anything unusual about me — at first — was when I was presented to the Mother Superior before Mass on the first Sunday after my arrival. It was late in the fall. I'd been sick with jaundice, and my father hadn't wanted me to leave home until my skin had lost its mustardy colour.

The Mother Superior didn't smile. She pressed her lips together in exactly the way I pictured nuns doing and she said, "She is unusually pretty, isn't she."

"She is Rosary Greening's younger sister, Mother," said the young nun beside me.

"Rosary Greening? O yes yes, of course. Well, she's entirely unlike Rosary Greening. What's your name, young lady?"

"Molly," I said.

The young nun murmured into my hair, "You must say 'Mother'."

I frowned. "Why? She's not my mother." My voice seemed to bounce around the dark wood of the big room and settle in the hollow of the empty fireplace.

The nun's eyes widened, but when I looked at the Mother Superior I thought maybe she was trying not to smile. "Now, young Molly Greening, your sister's the jewel of the establishment. I only hope you'll do us just as proud. Sister Bernadette, see Molly's hair is cut off." I went hot and cold all at once and the Mother Superior raised a hand. "It's the school policy, Molly. No vanities."

When they came at me with the scissors I bit one of them. But still nobody suggested I might be possessed by divine spirit.

I liked Sister Bernadette. After a few days I told her that every night I had dreams of being fed by the hands of angels. This was not strictly true, but it was the best way I could think of to suggest the subject of holy inheritance. Sister Bernadette looked at me with deep concern. "Really, Molly? That's very strange. Every night?"

My mother and father died in a car accident not two weeks after I entered St. Margaret's.

When I began school, Rosary was already at the teachers' college in the old seminary building. She came to visit me once every couple of weeks and looked terribly grown-up and distant. She didn't have to wear a uniform any longer, and although the older girls were allowed to grow their hair, hers was in a professional-looking little bob. She asked me a lot of motherly questions about my schoolwork and my friends. I didn't really have any friends except Sister Bernadette; the girls in my dormitory and my classes seemed stupid and coarse to me, and the couple of times I tried to elevate our conversation to matters more spiritual they laughed and looked frightened at the same time.

One day Rosary came for her regular second-Sunday visit and said she had something special to tell me. The Mother had given her permission to take me to lunch, and so we went to a café downtown and I ordered fish cakes. I remember that quite clearly. I don't know why I asked for fish cakes; we had them often at school, and I should have wanted something that was more of a treat. But if Rosary noticed she didn't say anything. I ordered a cup of coffee, and I thought she'd tell me I was too young for coffee; the Sisters didn't let us drink it. I didn't even like coffee. But she seemed far away.

During the meal she asked me a few questions, about my studies and how I was sleeping, but as I answered them she seemed to forget I was there.

After I asked the waiter for a rum cake for dessert, Rosary said, "Molly, I have something I need to tell you."

"I know." My mouth was full of coffee and some of it spilled on my blouse. I expected her to dip a napkin in her waterglass and dab it on the stain, but she didn't. "You said so before."

Rosary nodded. She was staring out the café window onto the cobblestones of the street. "Molly, I'm going to get married."

She hesitated as she said this, and so I knew it must be important, but I didn't know why. Rosary was nineteen, as far as I could remember, which seemed like the kind of age when people got married.

My rum cake arrived and I took a bite of it.

"My fiancé is a man from Ireland, and we'll be going there after the wedding. We won't have much money, Molly, so I don't know when I can come back to see you again. But once everything is settled in, I'll send for you and you can come and live with us on Inisheer."

I chewed my cake a bit. I'd never had rum anything before. I didn't like the flavour much.

"Aren't you going to be a teacher any more, then?" I asked.

Rosary shook her head. "No, Molly, not now. I'm going

to be a mother is what I'm going to be."

"Oh."

"The Sisters will take care of you here, Molly. You like it here, isn't that right?"

I pulled myself up straight. "I like being close to God."

Rosary's brow furrowed. "Yes. Well. We're not having a wedding as such. We don't want a fuss. But maybe you can come. I asked Mother Agnes and she said that, seeing as Colin and I will leave almost right after the ceremony, it'd be all right for you to be there, to say goodbye."

I hadn't finished my cake, but she signalled for the bill anyway.

The priest who married my sister to Colin Flaherty was named Father Bartholomew Corrigan.

You'd think that when you came along, the Sisters would finally have believed in my divinity. I hadn't even started bleeding. When I began to show, Mother Agnes called me to her room, slapped my face and demanded to know who the father was. I spat on her and explained that God was the father and would punish her for her brutality and lack of faith. I think this was the only thing that saved me from a beating; the Mother Superior looked so alarmed that Sister Bernadette was able to bustle me out of the room.

"Now Molly, really," Sister Bernadette whispered. "I know you're afraid, but we can't help you if you won't let us."

I soon stopped trying to explain, because I was tired, that I wasn't afraid and that I didn't need help.

I was moved out of the dormitory and into the seminary with the teachers-in-training. I didn't go to class any more. I sometimes spent whole days kneeling in prayer on the wooden floor by my bed, counting my ivory rosary until blisters rose on my fingertips; I would sit over my dinner with my eyes closed and my lips moving, not needing to eat. That soon changed; after a couple of months I was so ravenous that the only thing I could do was to stay on my knees in my room, chanting, until mealtime, when I would bolt everything in sight.

When I was five months gone, the Mother Superior called me to her chambers and sat me down in front of the fireplace. She told me Rosary had written and asked that I not be separated from my baby. "She's explained," the Mother said stiffly, with her hands folded on her knees and her eyes on the flames, "that once she and her husband are better established she'll bring you over to the Aran Islands to live with them. She's asked that in the meantime we keep both you and your child here and care for you. She insists this is what your parents, God rest their souls, would have wanted. I'm a little troubled, Molly, in that I'm not sure you have the … capacities necessary to care for a child. But the orphanage is, of course, dedicated to that very purpose. So I've decided we'll offer you and your sister a compromise. We'll turn your baby over to the orphanage and he'll be kept there until your sister is ready to accept you at her home. You'll return to your studies and to the normal life a twelve-year-old girl should be leading. Rosary has assured us that it'll not be long before she and her husband are established enough to provide for you and your child."

The Mother said some more things, but I didn't hear them. I placed my hands over my belly and I listened for God. It appeared that He had left me to my own devices. When the

Mother finished speaking, I nodded and waited for her to dismiss me. She seemed to expect something more, but in the end she let me go with a tired wave of her hand.

The one thing in all my life that has made me question my faith was the fact that you were born a girl. I was so shocked that I cried for several days after the birth. The nurse insisted it was common for new mothers to be sad, that giving birth was a terribly difficult and unsettling thing, that I'd be all right in time. What she didn't understand was that I knew I was being punished, and I didn't know why. I didn't know what I'd done to disappoint Him.

They let me live at the infirmary and breast-feed you for a few weeks, and for such a young girl I had a lot of milk, the nurses said. But they made me wean you too soon and whisked you away.

After you were gone a series of angels visited me while I slept, each night a different one: the dreams I'd told Sister Bernadette about had become real. But instead of feeding me they spoke to me. They told me I'd know, when the time came, what I was supposed to do.

Girls, I knew, were meant for sacrifice.

I named you Clare because your skin was so pale that I felt I could see right through to your bones.

You wouldn't remember much about the orphanage; you were still a baby the night I slipped in and carried you away.

The angel came to me, this time when I was awake, not asleep, and said God didn't need us any more. He didn't say why. Then he vanished. After my prayers I lay down on my bed — I was back in the dormitory then — lay until night trying to understand where I'd gone wrong. The other girls filed in, got ready for bed, and turned out the lights.

When it was very very dark and quiet, I got out of bed, slipped down the passage to the infirmary, sneaked past the nurse in her little booth, scooped you up, opened the first-floor window, and dropped outside with you in my arms.

It was a long walk, and a cold night, but God guided us all the way to the shore of Quidi Vidi Lake. On the way I didn't look around or think of what might be in the dark beyond the road; I just followed where He pointed me until I stepped out onto somebody's wharf with you in my arms. The water of the lake was black and thick, and I could feel the cold rising from it. I stood and watched the surface, because the surface was as far as I could see. I'd heard drowning was an easy, peaceful way to die. But then I looked along the beach and saw a fire burning.

I thought: *Maybe I heard the angel wrong. Maybe the angel said:* "You serve *another* purpose for God now. God has *another* plan for you." I watched the fire without moving. You didn't cry, even when I started to shiver; I think you were asleep. *This is a sure sign,* I thought. *I wasn't cold before and I'm cold now, so I should go to the fire.*

I turned back on the wharf and wandered down the beach toward the flames.

A man was sitting alone, staring into the fire and poking it with a long green branch. A halo of mist surrounded him and his fire in a bubble of dry heat. He looked up when I approached him and his face grew all surprised. He was around twenty years old and handsome, with dark hair and a deep, slanted look around his eyes. He reminded me a little of Father Bartholomew Corrigan.

"Jesus Mary and Joseph," he said softly.

I was even colder now, so I sat down near the fire with you still pressed against my chest. I looked straight into the flames and waited.

"What are you doing here, young miss?" he asked.

His voice was quiet and slow. I pushed my nose against your little neck and stretched my feet toward the warmth.

"God sent me here," I said.

"What?"

I didn't reply.

"Whose baby is that?"

"She's my baby."

I tried to imagine what his face was doing, but I didn't look at it. "Don't be foolish, now. You're not more than eleven or twelve years old. What's your name, darling?"

My heart was quiet. I tried to ask God, silently, what this man was here to do. God didn't seem to have anything to say to me.

"Molly Greening," I said. "This is Clare."

When I looked up his eyes were travelling up and down my body.

"Where do you live, Molly?"

I smiled. "We don't live anywhere now," I said.

He was good to you, Clare, do you remember? A good kind father. It was years before they found us. So close by, but I never left the house except in the dark, and I never went into town; he never had any visitors and I didn't need friends. When the police came to the door during those first weeks, I hid in an old refrigerator in the cellar; we were so sealed in that, even when you started to cry, they didn't hear a thing.

He could have left us in that refrigerator and let us die; it would have been easy; it happens to children all the time. He could have called the police a few days later, and said we did it ourselves, sneaked into his house and shut ourselves into the smelly dark. But he didn't do that. He risked everything for us. You were almost five years old when they finally took you away from me, and took him to jail. By that time all my hair had grown back again.

They've been trying all these years to tell me he was a bad man. But there are so few people who understand the ways of the Lord. Even I didn't understand them right away. I thought He was leading us to the shores of Quidi Vidi because He was done with us altogether. But that wasn't what He meant.

I didn't even mind it much. I liked the feeling of His body on top of mine, and I liked the sounds He made. I liked the way He would kiss and touch me afterwards.

Sometimes I'd look up and see you watching us from the doorway, your blue eyes almost milk-white.

The Cassatts said you were an angelic foster child. That was the word they used. *Angelic.* They said you were an excellent student, you did your chores around the house, your friends were all nice, sensible, upstanding children. You liked to read and to swim, and on weekends you often stayed home and played *Scrabble* or *Pictionary* with Mr. and Mrs. Cassatt and their friends. "She's so mature," Mrs. Cassatt told me, "so stable. She's never caused us a moment's worry. You'd never know .... " And she stopped herself.

I saw you about once a month. We went for drives once they let me have a car. We sat in the park. I asked you about boys, and school, and friends, and your new family, but you turned your blue eyes away, and answered yes and no. So I started taking you to the movies, where we didn't have to talk. It was more than I could afford on my bit of Welfare money, but I didn't know what else to do with you. I wanted to take you to church, but when I suggested it you looked at me horrified, like you were watching me lose an eye.

It was ten years before they let me have you again. I was twenty-seven, and you were almost fifteen. I stopped telling the psychiatrists about God and angels, and I took my medication. When I came to get you from the Cassatts, they cried, and so did you.

I'd come into my part of the inheritance, and now that I was no longer under hospital care I was allowed to use it. The social workers had found me a nice apartment. Rosary wanted me to come to Ireland, but the doctors and my counselor didn't think such a big change would be good, for either you or me. I didn't want to go either, not at first. But soon I started looking at atlases.

Our family is from there, Clare. They first came to Newfoundland from Ireland. Not from Inisheer where Rosary lives now, not even from County Galway. They came from County Clare. I remember that now, my father telling me long ago.

You could have been so pretty, with your dark curls and blue eyes and pale skin, but you could never quite lose those few pounds that would have made you perfect. You were a bit like Rosary had been when she was young, solid and dark, and your voice was like hers too, also solid and dark. You reminded me so much of Rosary when I first came to take you back. But then you began turning into someone else.

Maybe you were a good girl when you were with the Cassatts, but you weren't a good girl with me. You played hooky from school, and you smoked cigarettes. More than once, I came home from a church meeting to find you drinking beer in the apartment, with your friends and boyfriends. Sometimes you swore at me, when you spoke to me at all. You hardly looked at me most of the time. I prayed and prayed, but I could see you weren't interested in God's plan for you.

I didn't tell anyone we were leaving, not even you; I was afraid you'd tell your friends and my doctors would find out. I didn't even tell God. For all my efforts, God wasn't speaking to me.

When I got to Ireland the angels returned.

Michael Mulvaney had been a priest once. He was a heavy man with a black moustache, not tall, not handsome, but full of the Word. He told me I should stop taking the pills the doctors gave me and God would speak to me again.

The first time he tried to enter me on the beach on Inisheer, the angels came down and said: No. It is too late for you now, they said. You have been soiled. I cried when they told me that, remembering; I missed him still, that man who'd saved me. Michael was angry, and I understood that; he'd interpreted God's will differently. But I said, "Michael, it's not me, you see." And that's when I brought you to him.

"I believe, Michael," I said, "that she is still untouched."

I know you didn't understand, my honey. So many things had come between you and God. The only thing I doubted was whether it was right of me to watch. But Michael said he was sure God would tell me to go, if that was what he wanted. And through the whole night, God never said a word.

two

Clare

II

She must have told you by now. Wherever she is. Wherever you are, Auntie. I wish you'd answer me.

We've just taken off and below me the Atlantic is growing paler and smoother as we rise higher, the lace ribbons of foam becoming the texture of the whole, the way sand becomes as flat and featureless as paper unless you look at it from very close. The last time I covered this distance I was coming the other way, from there to here. It's the same ocean no matter what side you're on but the view of it is different somehow, depending. Familiar but different.

It's been five years now, almost exactly. I don't suppose she told you about that. I don't forget my promises, but I wasn't sure I'd go back until I found out I had a baby coming. My memories of you, of all that, didn't seem real any more, until the doctor said the words. Can you imagine, Auntie, me a mother? No, of course you can't, and you don't. You don't read my letters; you send them back to me with RETURN TO SENDER stamped on the envelope. I never thought you'd do that, return me to sender. But you did and you keep doing it. Unless it's not you at all.

I still hardly remember if you want to know the truth, Auntie. I hardly remember what Inisheer looks like even. Rocks mostly, and I remember the castle ruins.

I remember the boat coming up on the pier, and looking out to see the big sign saying *FLAHERTY'S B&B*. Even if I hadn't known *FLAHERTY'S B&B* was where I was going I might have thought for a second that it was the only place to go because that painted sign was so big, so bright and green and white with the curlicues and flowers like a place you'd like to go, a place full of curlicues and flowers where you could lay your head down and it would float away on a pillow of the best things in Ireland. The best things. Maybe you were the best thing in Ireland, Auntie. Maybe you were the best thing in the whole world.

When Mumma and I stepped off the boat from Galway onto the pier of Inisheer the sky was as white-grey as the edges of the sea. And I could only do what I was told no matter how much I wanted to throw myself into the wake of the *Aran Flyer* and follow it all the way back to Galway or until I drowned.

Seams of perfect stone stitches stretched all up and down as far as the land went, dividing it into bits and streams of green. The houses all jostling together to greet me: Over here! No no little Clare over here! And Mumma with her feet heavy on the dock, her piles of butter-gold hair heavy in the air, looking up with a smile as if the houses were calling to her and not to me at all.

"We're here, my honey," she said.

I half expected — I realize it now — a fat and laughing You to be standing on the steps of *FLAHERTY'S B&B* wiping your hands on your apron and calling "Top o' the mornin' to you!" But not only was it well past noon and not morning at all but there didn't seem to be anyone anywhere up and down the pier road. The outside of *FLAHERTY'S B&B* was white and cold and still as a lily in a florist's fridge with all its pollen pulled out.

Mumma reached out a hand and took mine. "Rosary's waiting for us, my honey," she said.

I picked up the satchel that one of the boat-hands had tossed out at my feet and Mumma led me up the little path to *FLAHERTY'S B&B* as though I were five, and I allowed myself to be led as though I were five.

You weren't fat. You were boney and big and warm-faced and although you were wearing a greying apron you didn't wipe your hands on it. You were standing over the stove in the kitchen when we came in, taking a boiling kettle off the heat. As you turned toward the door I saw beads of steam or sweat on your wide brown forehead.

You said, "Hello Molly dear," with no expression, but fixed your black eyes on me and almost smiled. "You must be Clare," you said. The kitchen was scattered with dishes, open bags of sandwich bread, grease. The smell was of teabags and fried potatoes. Through the windows was the sea, salt grey.

You took me upstairs to Gilly's room right away, leaving Mumma to sit in the kitchen. I remember Gilly's room all yellow and her in yellow too, a yellow t-shirt, and me too, in the yellow dress Mumma bought me in Galway, clingy and almost all the way to the floor. On the boat I'd pulled the neckline of that dress down to show my tits to the boat-hand who kept staring at me all the way over. He turned even redder than his sunburn, almost brown he was so red. I still have that yellow dress; I almost left it behind in Gilly's room when you sent me home at the end of the summer — something for Gilly to remember me by — but thinking of the boat-hand I finally packed it up. And when I was getting ready, late last night when the Cassatts were asleep, I put the yellow dress in my bag, took it out, put it back in. I don't know if I'll wear it but I felt somehow it should come with me.

I remember looking at Gilly and thinking there must be

some mistake. From the back I could see only her long black sheet of hair and her boney brown upper arms as her elbows rested on the window sill, but even from that angle she looked Chinese, and how could I have a Chinese cousin? She kept staring out the window while you left and went downstairs, and I sat on the bed next to her and asked her if she had a cigarette. I thought maybe that would shock her — she looked so fragile and pretty from behind — but she turned her face to me and I saw she had freckles and her slant eyes were blazing like jars full of sparks.

She was like that — sparks caught in a skinny jar. I learned that later. I learned she was afraid to let herself out, she was afraid of the things she knew she was capable of.

She reached under the bed and pulled out a pack of Silk Cuts and opened the window and she lit both our cigarettes and we hung our hands outside. When the cigarettes were almost done we waited for tourists to pass under the window so we could drop the burning butts on their heads, but you called us to dinner before any came.

I remember the sun didn't seem to set until it was almost morning. Every night.

We slept together in her bed in her yellow room when we slept at all. In the beginning, when we first arrived, at night I'd hear Gilly's door open and I'd slide my eyes awake a crack and Mumma would be standing there watching me, her gold hair all lit from behind like a house of glass on fire, her face a gaping shadow. Gilly would be breathing deep sleep beside me. I'd watch Mumma watch us and I never knew if she knew that I knew. Then she'd go away and the door would close behind her. Sometimes I'd move closer to Gilly as though I thought such a little bundle of bones could do anything to save me. She was so tiny and breakable in the light from the moon outside; sometimes after Mumma'd gone I'd just lie awake watching the breath move Gilly's face. In the daytime her face was hard and sharp and bright like a polished gold vault, but at night its surface was thin as the skin of a bodhran.

O the bodhran. Well you know all about bodhrans, having lived on Inisheer all these years. Are you still there, Auntie? If you're still there why do you keep returning me to sender? I started learning the bodhran when I got back that summer; the only thing I could think of was finding someone to teach me how to hit that drum. I did finally, a woman at the music school who took pity on me and agreed to tutor me for free. She let me join her Celtic band. We play at the hotels sometimes; I even made some money that way. It all went into my Ireland fund. Everything went into the fund. Into Ireland. I didn't even buy my own bodhran; my teacher lent me one of hers and then told me to keep it.

The bodhran's fun. Rhythm's the thing; I've always liked that.

Were you there that night Teffia and her father danced in the hotel pub? I don't remember if you were there or not. It was the first time I'd seen a bodhran. As I watched that drummer cantering away on the thing I felt the vibrations travelling from the soles of my feet and the palms of my hands right into my solar plexus, shivering and shimmering there like a bud about to burst.

(My teacher told me that the word *bodhar* means haunting. Imagine that, Auntie.)

When Michael Mulvaney came into the hotel pub with Mumma that night I was already drunk and the sight of him made me scared and queasy all over. I'd never seen him before, even though his daughter sang there three nights a week. He was a greasy man with a puffy black moustache, short and fat and dart-eyed. Teffia's mother must have been the beauty queen of Inisheer for Teffia to turn out the way she did. Maybe Michael wasn't her father at all. But Teffia's tendency to have sex with everything must have come from somewhere. Her father was likely to have given her that.

He and Mumma sat by the window and I wondered who he was. Teffia had finished her singing for the evening and was propped next to the fiddler, chewing a fingernail and gazing toward the doorway. There was a storm beginning outside, a rumbling out over the water. Then the fiddle started thin as mist and the whistle followed.

I wish when they came to the floor and he began to spin her and the crowd spread away to give them the space they needed, I wish it had been horror or quiet discomfort that filled the room and pressed against the thunder outside. I wish a heavy silence had settled over us as we watched Teffia and the black-haired man stamping and swirling with her red hair flying and her white dress — it was always a white dress, all her white dresses over and over — her white dress wrapping and clinging around her knees, with his stubby greasy fingers light and firm on her whispers of hips.

But it wasn't like that. The pub began clapping, the old boat-hands at the bar and the Dutch couple at the window and everyone else except the musicians, whose hands were busy, and Mumma who sat silent, the straw from her Coke between her lips, looking about twelve years old. The fiddler knew just how vicious a fiddle could be. He scratched and bit and the whistle blurted for the bodhran to do something. The bodhran woke up and the fiddle was pissed and everyone clapped and the bodhran let rip with a tatatattatattatatumtumtumtum whistles and strings and shouts of joy hammers hitting everything imaginable and if this hotel doesn't blow right into the sky then we'll drive it into the ground with the pounding of feet under tables shaking the windows. The heavy door blew open and rain shattered across the floor and we could hear through the music the sea and the thunder yelling.

Teffia and the black-haired man laughed to one another. The man's fat face grew bright as lightning and his feet fluttered like birds through the wash of rain on the wood. Teffia's hair ran like a pale river stained with blood and she looked up into his eyes with the delight Gilly might feel at the Second Coming.

We all laughed and clapped and shouted for them. That is, everyone around me did. I'm not sure what I was doing. The reel went on and on and on building and racing and the sweat soaked them like the rain and if we thought they were done someone pounded on again and the bodhran laughed at them each time they thought they could rest, until finally with a great shout from us all Teffia collapsed into the black-haired man's laughing arms.

Gilly and I went home together early that night; she and Teffia must have been fighting and I didn't really want to tell Niall no once again. (I was working up to yes.) Gilly and I lay in bed and I asked who that man with Mumma was, the man who danced with Teffia. "O that's Teffie's father, Michael," Gilly said. "Your mother would do well to stay away from him."

Where were you? In the kitchen waiting for the world to fall down? Why didn't you tell Mumma to stay away from Michael Mulvaney? Why didn't you tell your daughter and your niece not to stay out until six in the morning getting wasted and fucking and falling off the pier? Gilly did that once, fell off the pier into the greasy littered water; we had to hold Teffia by the ankles so she could pull her out. Teffia was surprisingly strong.

In the nights after that first time I saw her and Michael together, Mumma came home rumpled and still breathing hard like she'd been running, but running with her whole body, her skin tender and slightly blue all over where every point of her had touched the ground. I lay awake for hours until she opened the bedroom door and looked in, standing in the doorway with the light behind her, her face a black hole, hair like dandelion seed in the sun. There was always a hint even in silhouette of clothes in disarray, the fragility of pounded skin, and always I could hear how quick and strong and turbulent her breath was, like a storm on the way.

When the door closed behind her I felt sick with the memory of Mulvaney's fat hands, and then sicker with the memory of his feet and face dancing as quick and brilliant as doves.

I don't remember that night Mumma came to take me to the beach. No, I do remember, but not the part when she came, not the part when we were going. Gilly told me after; I have a picture in my mind of me sleepwalking in my white nightgown, gliding over the rocks like Jesus on water, not slipping once. And Mumma ahead of me in a pale pink sleeveless shift, looking neither left nor right, angelic and certain. I can picture these things because Gilly told me. But I don't remember. How could I? Why would I follow my mother halfway around Inisheer in the middle of the cold night, nothing on my feet, not knowing where I was going or why? Why would I do anything my mother asked me to?

I suppose I must have sleepwalked all the way to Ireland too.

I'm on my way to the *Plassy* again, and the ocean has disappeared below the clouds. It's a nice feeling, knowing that something can come between me and the sea.

I had a dream last night. I climbed down stones to sit by a river, and when I got there I had something in my hand. I hadn't had it when I climbed down, and holding it I wouldn't be able to climb up. But it was important and I couldn't leave it behind. I tried to take it back up with me but I dropped it and it fell into the river. The river took it away. But I don't remember what it was. I'm not sure I even knew at the time.

THREE

Gillian

III

I have heard many such things: miserable comforters are ye all.

Shall vain words have an end? or what emboldeneth thee that thou answerest?

I also could speak as ye do: if your soul were in my soul's stead, I could heap up words against you, and shake mine head at you.

But I would strengthen you with my mouth, and the moving of my lips would asswage your grief.

Though I speak, my grief is not asswaged: and though I forbear, what am I eased?

He breaketh me with breach upon breach, he runneth upon me like a giant.

I have sewed sackcloth upon my skin, and defiled my horn in the dust.

My face is foul with weeping, and on my eyelids is the shadow of death.

O earth, cover not thou my blood, and let my cry have no place.

Also now, behold, my witness is in heaven, and my record is on high.

My friends scorn me: but mine eye poureth out tears unto God.

That's in Job. Chapter Sixteen. Look it up, Clary darling.

FOUR

Clare

IV

Auntie, where are you? The woman who owns the B&B now is making me pay.

Nothing's really changed here except now the sign says *INIS OIRR BED AND BREAKFAST* without the flowers and curlicues, and I'm staying in a guest room. I saw that same boat-hand on the *Aran Flyer*, the one I showed my tits to the last time I came over. He's a bit older but I'm pretty sure it's him, his freckled pug face brown and sheep-eyed. I wonder if I'd worn my yellow dress would it have brought something back to him, would he have had a sudden bewildering embarrassment of a hard-on and a mental flash of fifteen-year-old fat peach boobs.

That yellow dress might stay in my bag. I'm afraid the baby pushing my belly out will show.

The B&B woman doesn't know a thing about you, or that's what she says. She's only been here a few years, married into the island just like you, Auntie. But she told me that Gilly lives over in the castle village, and that she had the post officer put all your letters in Gilly's post box. So it must have been Gilly who's been returning me to sender all these years. I wrote to say I was coming, but maybe she returned that one too and it's on its way to Newfoundland. Maybe I passed it over the Atlantic.

Every now and then, walking around the roads from the B&B to the shops to the pub to the beach and back again, I saw a face that seemed to know me. But it's been a long time and I've grown my hair and I'm swelling a bit with baby, so it's not hard to be invisible, an American girl they think, one of the hundreds who gallop through this place looking for some scent of where they came from.

I went up to the hotel pub in the afternoon. There was a fat freckled young man behind the bar who I thought I recognized, but I couldn't think of a name. He told me Niall still works there but only in the evenings, so I left and took a walk along the beach near the pier. There were small children playing in the cold foam and a bunch of pre-teen students from the Irish school, yelling and laughing in English and Irish all mixed together in a way that upset me; it's an unfair advantage, having more than one language. One young man alone, a blond man with thin legs in shorts, ran barefoot all along the crest of the surf from the pier down to the airstrip, then back again, then back again. I sat down on the sand for a while and watched him.

As I was strolling today, I was telling my belly some stories. I do that sometimes. I sat on the sand watching the blond man gallop back and forth, and I told my belly about how Gilly and I once swam naked just out there, in the very last hours of the night. (She loved to get wet once she had a few drinks in her, I told my belly.) She started tearing off her clothes before we even left the road, so I did too, and when we plunged in we screamed with the cold and then she started to laugh and laugh — drink always made everything funny for her — until I couldn't help but laugh too. There was phosphorescence on the water that night, and when we lifted our arms out of the foam they glowed with a sheen of living light. Gilly scooped up a little jellyfish in her hands, so completely transparent that we wouldn't have seen it if it hadn't been for the splash of shimmering blue entrails at its heart. Then the sun coming up surprised us and we ran out onto the sand and watched the sky go all shades of marigold. I cared if someone saw us standing shivering with our clothes strewn from the road all the way to the water, but Gilly didn't.

I can see the ocean and that ribbon of beach from where I'm sitting now at my window, grey and white as seagulls. The sun still doesn't set here, I see. At least not until the night is almost over.

I started reading the Bible because of her. I've stopped again now but for a while I read a bit every day. All those years I wouldn't because Mumma kept trying to make me. But I saw the red *King James* on Gilly's bedside table as we were getting ready for bed the first night when I arrived. "Are you religious?" I asked her and she said with a blazing smile — O, Auntie, you know — she said, "No, just Catholic. But I like the words in *King James* best." And I said, "Are there Catholics in China?" And she said, "You are an ignorant cow. I was born in Japan, but I am Irish and therefore Catholic."

"Do you believe in God?" I asked and she smiled again. Her skin was like moonlight on wet sand.

"I do," she said. "There's no harm in it."

"No harm in God?"

Gilly laughed, showing little white teeth. "There's plenty of harm in God. That's what I like in Him." I sat down on the bed and picked up the Bible. "Start with Ecclesiastes," she said.

We slept together in that little bed of hers almost every night, in her room that's closed to me now that I'm a guest. Sometimes I woke up to find her very close. I never really understood until I met Teffia. That wasn't until a few days later. Gilly took me up to the hotel pub to watch the band and Teffia was singing. She probably wasn't old enough to be singing in a bar but Gilly and I weren't old enough to be drinking in one either; Niall the bartender slipped us half-pints of Guinness in Coke glasses and scooped the foam off, made us drink it with straws, as if everyone there didn't know the difference — it was really for your sake, Auntie.

If Mumma was the prettiest woman in the history of the world, Teffia would've had to be next, don't you think? Seeing her in her white dress with her strawberry hair all the way down her back, I thought jealousy might shoot that Guinness right out of my mouth and all over the pub floor. And I saw how Gilly was looking at her. It was so thick I couldn't believe everyone in the bar wasn't choking in it.

You liked Teffia in spite of yourself, I know you did. One afternoon I passed the front room and she was in there with you; you hadn't told Gilly and me that she'd arrived. You were playing something on the piano from some sheet music that she must have brought along — a pop song; Celine Dion maybe. And she was next to you on the stool singing, softly but it made the house hum like a window pane when a semi passes far away. I poked my head in and the two of you looked up and I saw a trace of your smile, which was not coming but going, as though you wanted to put it away before I understood that Teffia was all right by you. Even if you pinched your lips when you saw her and Gilly leaving the house walking so close that their clothes brushed together, Teffia was still all right by you.

That first evening when Gilly took me to the hotel pub Teffia was singing boney when we came in. I knew that one. Mrs. Cassatt used to sing it around the house sometimes when I was young, but nothing like that. I couldn't believe the band members could keep playing and not stop in shame. Not that they were bad, just that it seemed wrong for anything else to happen while that singing was going on. Her eyes were closed and it slipped out of her in soft trembling waves like heartbreak was swelling up under her white skin and cracking through at her throat.

Niall slid our glasses to us as we sat down and nobody said a word. The bar was silent, packed with Americans and Germans and French and Dutch, but mostly with the locals who came every night and tore the place up with their Irish and their bellowing but who sat like stone birds listening to Teffia Mulvaney sing.

When she was done the song the band packed up their instruments for a while and she slid into the seat beside Gilly's. Gilly was a twig beside her and Teffia was a tree, a birch tree blooming with roses. Side by side on the bartop their arms were boney, milk-cream and beach-brown, Teffia's long and soft-muscled, Gilly's crackable, a splinter. Beside them I felt like a scrubbed cherub bulging in all directions.

Gilly muttered something in Irish at Teffia and Teffia muttered something back at her and they both laughed. Teffia looked across at me. Gilly said, "This is my cousin Clare from Canada. Clare, this is Teffia," and I nodded. Teffia's singing had curdled inside me with the Guinness and with the sight of her arms next to Gilly's on the counter, just touching.

(Don't call it love, not any of it. That's such a hollow word. And desire is too heavy. Call it want. That says it all. *I want* ... I am lacking. I want you: I lack you. I would make a soup but I want meat to flavour it. I would make a life but I want you. And you. Many nights later I understood, when Teffia and her father almost broke the floor dancing on it. Sometimes we want something so badly that we grab and hold on with everything we have, even if we seem to barely graze it around the waist with our fingertips.)

Later that first night, when all the singing and drinking was over, Niall locked up the bar and took the three of us, Gilly and Teffia and me, up the hill to the ruins of the O'Brien castle where a bunch of other boys were sitting around, and we smoked weed and drank some Bulmer's cider. That castle loomed above me the whole day today as I walked, but I didn't go up although I want to see it, more than anything else, I think, all falling down and open to the world, except for that one black room in the centre where there's stone still standing the whole way around and one tiny sightless door. The outside walls that have crumbled into steps perfect for climbing up to the top. The way the wind tears at you from up there, trying to knock you around, making it hard to hear anything else, even the person who's beside you. That first night I ended up climbing the castle wall with Niall and getting sick over the side while he held my hair back off my face and laughed.

He was a nice boy, Niall. Not a boy really, almost twenty, and I guess it wasn't very gallant of him to kiss fifteen-year-old girls but he was a gentleman, never did a thing until I rinsed my puke-slick mouth with some more cider and planted one on him. He didn't resist even though I'd just been throwing my guts up. His hair was almost the same colour as the moon. We kissed for a while on the top of that broken castle wall with the wind trying to throw us off and even through the cider haze I felt something. Then he walked me home. The sun was coming up and there was no one around but us, and when he got me to the door of the B&B I put my hands up inside his shirt and he put his up mine, but that was all I allowed and he didn't seem to mind.

By that time all the other boys had gone home too and Gilly and Teffia were left alone in the castle. It was hours before Gilly got home.

(Even then I didn't get it. I didn't get it until one afternoon many weeks later. The three of us were sitting out on the rocks facing away from Ireland and toward home. Gilly and Teffia had been spitting at one another in Irish until finally Gilly ran away along the beach. I never asked what those fights were all about. Gilly never talked to me about Teffia. And I hated the Irish language, felt somehow that all of Ireland was conspiring to keep me in the dark — I didn't know then that hardly anyone in Ireland speaks Irish any more, that places like Inisheer are the ones outside the world.

Teffia sat stone-like staring out over the ocean for a while. Then she turned to me and tried to kiss me and took my hand and put it up her white dress. She had no underwear and she was all damp and smooth. All right, it's true, I let her, although I wouldn't let her kiss me. She lay back on the rocks and undid the front of her dress so I could see her white plum freckled breasts falling away from each other and I rubbed her, watching her face. She came in about sixty seconds screaming and thrashing like a dervish, her voice bouncing off all the greyness of the rocks and the water. I'd never seen anything like it. Then she scrambled off without even buttoning her dress, a white and copper speck carried away on the wind, and I had to walk back over the rocks alone. I didn't see a soul.

Gilly never left us alone together again.

I once asked Niall if he'd ever had sex with Teffia and he said, "Clary darling, there wouldn't be a man on this island who hasn't been with Teffia Mulvaney." He raised his blond eyebrows in what I knew was a meaningful expression. Not until I saw Michael Mulvaney did I understand. No, not even then.

Gilly didn't come home, that morning after we'd been in the castle, until well after you were fixing breakfast; I woke up when she crept into the bedroom and you were already clanging around in the kitchen. When she slipped past the kitchen door did you call "Good morning, Gillian" in that clipped quiet voice of yours? Because when I was up and she and I'd both showered and dressed, her without sleeping and me feeling I hadn't, and we both came and sat at the breakfast table, made sick at the smell of sausages and eggs, and we drank some orange juice and made a show of pouring Corn Flakes and milk but stirred everything around without speaking, you said, "You girls are looking like death on a plate, go back to bed for the love of God." That was all. There were many nights and mornings after when it happened just like that.

She never went to the church with you and you didn't seem to care. Perhaps you thought that with all her Bible reading she was getting enough God. I'd surprise her in her room where she'd be sitting up on the bed next to the open window, a cigarette in one hand and *King James* in the other. It scared me. But Gilly seemed so true about it. Sometimes she'd read me little bits. "Listen to this, Clary Sage," she'd say. (The first time she called me Clary Sage I said, "My name's not Clarisage," but she explained that it's an herb that causes euphoria. She knew all about herbs and things. I used to look at her collection of mysterious little bottles that she bought in Galway, with their white labels — jasmine, bergamot, lavender, melissa, rockrose, neroli, eucalyptus, hyssop, immortelle, myrtle, ylang-ylang, tea tree, clary sage — and wonder.)

She'd say, "Listen to this, Clary Sage. 'And whatsoever mine eyes desired I kept not from them, I withheld not my heart from any joy. Then I looked on all the works that my hands had wrought, and on the labour that I had laboured to do: and behold all was vanity and vexation of spirit.' Ecclesiastes Two, Verses Ten and Eleven."

And I'd say, "Okay." And she'd say, "Don't you see?" And I'd say, "What?" And she'd say, "O don't trouble yourself." And I'd say, "No, what?" But she wouldn't answer me. And a day later we'd have the same conversation again. "'My son, eat thou honey, because it is good; and the honeycomb, which is sweet to thy taste: so shall the knowledge of wisdom be unto thy soul: when thou hast found it, then there shall be a reward, and thy expectation shall not be cut off.' Proverbs Twenty-Four, Verses Thirteen and Fourteen."

And I'd say, "Okay." And she'd say, "Don't you see? That's just the opposite of what it was saying yesterday." And I'd say, "No, what?"

And so on. It was like she was talking to herself. I was just as happy. It didn't matter to me as long as she didn't send me away.

She would sit with her legs in her cut-off shorts splayed like a wishbone, the Good Book on the bed inches from her crotch, her other hand with a Silk Cut between her finger-bones hanging out the window. All her sheet of black hair hanging around her. She'd move over so I could smoke out the window too and we'd sit not quite touching, she reading the Word of the Lord and me thinking.

But she never went to church and of course neither did I. We'd spend Sunday mornings sleeping off the sickest hangovers I've ever had. Guinness and Bulmer's cider; what was I thinking? Not much, I suppose. I feel like I spent all my time thinking, but when I try to remember what was going through my head it seems like an endless blank, like snow on a television, noisy but empty.

I'm trying to imagine what Gillian looks like now and can't picture her any different than she was: whip of hair and freckles like an oil spatter, limbs thin as pencils.

I keep thinking of this story you told me about Tchaikovsky, one day when I was sitting at the piano in your front room: Tchaikovsky was obsessed by the tonic chord, the chord that signals without a doubt that the piece is over.

dum dadada dum dum dummmmmm

DINK!

That last

DINK!

is the tonic chord. When T was a child and lying in his bed at night his older sister would play the piano downstairs. And to torture him she'd finish her piece without the tonic chord.

dum dadada dum dum dummmmmm

And little T would lie with his teeth grinding until finally he had to get out of bed and go downstairs and slam on the keys.

DINK!

I've felt that tooth-grinding ever since I went home from Inisheer. Now I've come back to slam on the keys but the piano's gone. Little T's sister sold it to someone across town and now I'm sitting where it used to be with my spine crawling up and down.

Late in the afternoon today I went around to the souvenir shops and bought an Aran sweater — not a handknit one, I can't afford that, but a pretty black cardigan made at the knitwear factory on Inishmaan. I looked at knotwork rings like the copper one Niall bought me in Galway, the day before he took me to Shannon Airport and put me on the plane home. I lost that ring down a drain this spring. It turned my finger green but I wore it for five years. Down the drain in the locker room shower at the gym where I went to do yoga. I went back a few times to stand in that stall, over that drain, hoping to feel some tarnishing copper loneliness travelling back up the pipes. In the shop I thought about buying another one but didn't.

This is only the second time I've been anywhere all alone. The first was those six hours on the plane from Shannon back to Newfoundland and to the Cassatts. I'm looking out this window which looks out over the sea, and although it's almost night the birds are circling in the pale light and the tourists are still wandering the sand with their children and their rolled cuffs. I can hear music from the pub next door, not the hotel pub but the other one, not the kind of music they play at the hotel but American pop music coming from a stereo. And I think: what if I went down into that pub and sat at a table until someone tried to talk to me? What if they followed me home and tossed me down on the dirt under my window?

I could walk over to Gilly's house and bang on her door but I think I need some time. The B&B woman says Gilly lives in a green house and makes incense for some hippie shop in Galway and never speaks to anyone. No one knows a thing about her except that Teffia goes up to see her. Why are they still here? After everything wouldn't Gilly want to be somewhere else?

Maybe that's what happened to you. You wanted to be somewhere else.

Teffia still sings at the hotel pub three nights a week, the barman said.

V

It was eleven tonight when I went up to the hotel pub. He was wiping things down, his thick tail of white-blond hair brushing the countertop. I sat in front of him and waited for him to recognize me, but it was a minute before he even saw me, as he bustled up and down the bar answering the Irish shouts that began with "Niall!" and continued into something I wished I could fathom.

He doesn't look much older. A little thicker but still skinny. He was never handsome, Niall, but he carries himself like a beautiful man, tossing around his wavy hair the colour of the inside of a birch tree, walking with his head high as though his pocked skin and crooked teeth were all a part of his charm. Gilly told me that every summer he chose a visiting beauty or two or three. (I'd seen some of those beauties sitting at the bar, letting their long slim fingers drape over his side of it, smiling wanly with a tilt of their blond heads. He looked at them exactly the same way he looked at me, at least in the beginning. I knew I wasn't one of those coy thin-fingered girls with their pert small breasts and their scent of expensive perfume and their firm legs in their hotel-ironed walking shorts, so I wondered what good I was to him.) "Your man's quite a prize," Gilly told me, "they fight over him."

"But you don't."

"Not me. He's like a brother to me. Looks out for me, doesn't let anyone take the piss out of me because of my chink face. He's a good boy, himself, he's kind."

One night when Niall was at the bar and the rest of us were sitting around it, Gilly told one of the boys to fuck off and he called her a chink dyke twat. Niall's eyes rose slowly from the pint he was pulling and froze on the boy for several long seconds. A hot blush rose in the boy's face and he gave a terse giggle. Niall's glass-blue eyes didn't waver; his jaw shifted. The boy spat, "For the love of Christ, Niall, we're all friends here." Niall was motionless except for a quick release of his hand from the beer tap. Finally the boy muttered, "All right, Gilly, forgive my insolence." "And you mine," she said absently, her eyes on Niall. Niall's eyes closed and he picked up the pint and moved off down the bar to someone who'd been waiting too long for his drink.

Niall once said to me, one of those nights when we were alone in the castle and I hadn't yet worked up to saying yes, he said to me, "The boys are starting to think you're of Gilly and Teffie's kind." And I asked, "What does that mean?" And he said, "O surely you know."

I suppose that decided me, because the next night I said yes to him. He was my first. I woke up in the middle of the night and couldn't go to sleep again; the ocean was too loud. Gilly was barely breathing, her face breakable in sleep. I slipped out of bed, pulled on my jeans and tiptoed down the stairs and out of the house.

I'd been dreaming about the graveyard at the foot of the hill, about a stone with Mumma's name on it sprouting like a mushroom from the middle of the ruins of the sunken temple of Saint Kevin. The temple is like a cellar, the walls still pressed up against the earth but the roof gone, exposing the stone entrails and the earthen floor to the sky and the dead people above.

As I approached I could hear panting and giggling. I peered over the edge of the ruin down into the hollow in the ground surrounded by crumbling tombstones only to see Niall's head of long hair glowing silver by the moon, on top of some girl spread on the earth. I pulled myself back and listened for a bit. They moaned and shuffled and my insides grew tighter and sharper every second.

They gave no sign of finishing soon, so I wandered down to the beach and tossed some rocks in the water. It was a warmish clear night and the stars were dull and half-asleep. I tried unsuccessfully to skip a couple of stones across the surface of the waves.

One day a few years before, Mumma had taken me out to a beach at Cape Spear in the middle of winter and tried to teach me to skip rocks. I was about eleven. We'd had to wade through snow almost waist-high to reach the beach, but it was easy to walk once we got there because the sea had washed the sand clean and hard. We picked up the smooth stones and tossed them side-armed over the sea, trying to spin them with our fingers. She was perfect with hers — they skimmed the water like birds — but mine all sank, as stones are supposed to. I fired them into the foam a few times and then gave up. The sea was slate-grey and howled like a mother who'd lost all her babies.

I turned to look at Mumma but she didn't see me. She was looking out toward Ireland. She said, "Someday, my honey, you and me are going to go there and live with Rosary. And we'll be happy there. We'll be very very happy, and God will take care of us."

For a quick guilty moment I wanted to throw the stone in my hand at her golden head and crack it open. She didn't see me as I stared at her and she didn't ask what I was thinking; she gazed out over the ocean. I decided then and there that I was never going to promise anyone anything for as long as I lived unless I was absolutely sure I could make that promise true.

I left Mumma at the edge of the water and walked by myself down the beach. All along it I found tiny orange shells, little snail shells all the same coral colour, no bigger each one of them than the head of a match. I had to dig them out of the packed sand with a fingernail or sift through piles of frozen pebbles. I found myself a pocket full of them. Near the tideline there was a puddle in a cold hollow where the sea had just washed in and I dropped the whole mess of shells into it and watched them deepen from coral-peach to apple-red. I left them but when I got home I missed them and cried. I thought of asking her to take me back there again one day but I didn't. I tried never to ask my mother for anything.

Anytime we were near the sea she'd look out over it, her hair whipping into a tangle of gold, and she'd say, "We've never been there, Clare. We'll go together some day. That's where Rosary is."

And now, I thought as I threw some more stones and waited for the girl under Niall to go away, *Mumma's kept her promise.* That was the astonishing thing. But we weren't here together, exactly. We'd arrived and she'd somehow disappeared, retreated into the house with her angels. This was before Michael Mulvaney, or before I knew about him in any case. But she'd already gone somewhere I couldn't follow.

Or was it me, perhaps, who'd gone somewhere, gone off into Gilly's world of Bulmer's cider and skinny-dipping as the sun came up? Of kissing in the ruins of castles and sex in graveyard temples? If it was me, though, Mumma'd done nothing to stop me. She was busy.

I pitched one last rock into the ocean and looked back toward the graveyard as the girl, also blond although not platinum-silver like Niall, climbed back to the world, straightened her clothes, stumbled a little and headed up the hill toward the hotel.

Niall was alone on one of the sunken stone walls smoking a joint, his hair a pale echo of the moon on the sea, a litre of cider beside him three-quarters gone. He looked up, smiled in a friendly way as if I'd dropped by his kitchen for tea and a chat, gesticulated with the joint. I climbed over and sat next to him, took the joint and drew on it. The smoke burned my lungs and made me cough. I spat into the temple and he smiled again, this time as if I were a baby learning to walk.

"What brings you out among the dead in the middle of the night, Clare? Don't you know the spirits are walking?" His voice flinted, stones on stones.

"Spirits like you, you mean?" I stretched out on my back along the wall, my head away from him, my calves dangling on either side.

He laughed. "Aye, let's call me a spirit. I like that. Would it make me safe?"

I wanted to be careless but my voice was fragile as a sprain. "Safe how? I like dangerous things."

He leaned back on his hands and turned his face to the sky. I've never, before that or since, seen anyone so self-possessed, so sure that whatever he was doing was just fine. Do you remember, Auntie, one afternoon in your kitchen when I told you that Irish people seemed certain to me, that they seemed not to ask themselves questions? Always facing me and looking me square in the eye, ready to laugh if I suggested there was an answer other than the one they were giving. You smiled wryly and said, "They look that way, don't they now."

"You like dangerous things, do you," he said softly to the moon. "You don't strike me that way, I must say. You look like a spoiled cat, plump and white as you are."

I snorted. "You're one to talk. Sitting here with the only people who can't cause you any harm."

"Can't you cause me any harm?" He smiled and took a swig of cider. Then he turned his face, lit on one side and dark on the other, toward me, his hair a brook of silver, his eyes grey and glittering as stones under water. I had heard people say this before, Auntie, but it was the first time I ever felt it: my heart leapt in my chest.

We didn't speak for a minute. I watched the warm breeze push at the stars and I pulled at the joint. After a moment I felt him shuffle. *Impatient,* I thought, *wanting to go home to bed maybe.*

"Don't you think," I asked, puffing some more, "that a little privacy is in order when you're fucking the tourists' daughters?"

He paused for a moment, then chuckled and tossed his hair although it wasn't in his face and so needed no tossing. "O, so you've seen that. I apologize." He slid along the wall toward me and held his hand out for the joint.

I slapped the hand away. Then I took another hit and handed it back. His amusement dissolved and he gazed into my face with a seriousness that made me wriggle.

He sighed and nodded slowly. "I see." His voice was almost penitent. "Forgive me, Clare, but you haven't been forthcoming, and I am not a man with marrying intentions. I like you, though. If you don't want me to be fucking the tourists' daughters, perhaps I can abstain until you've gone home." He handed me the bottle of cider. "You are a tourist's daughter yourself, though; you might remember that."

I sat up and shrugged, swigged the last of the cider and wiped my mouth with the back of my hand. I dropped the empty bottle into the depths of the temple, watched it bounce and roll and lie still, the moon glinting off its brown surface.

The golden face of my mother asleep somewhere in your B&B washed over me. I didn't even know — I still don't know — whether she was in fact asleep, whether she was protected by your roof and your walls. And by you. That's what I was thinking the whole time we were there, until the end; I was thinking that you were keeping her safe just by cooking her fry-ups that she didn't eat and by watching her as she moved in and out of the door that led to the pier. I thought without knowing I thought it that you'd taken the place of the angels. I know now that it wasn't you. But I wished it so much that I believed it to be true.

Niall was waiting for me to say something, to do something. I sent my mother away. I didn't want the gold burst of her hair filling my head. I wanted completely sightless black and his hands in all the right places and parts of him where no one had been before.

"I want to go up to the castle," I said.

His face was in shadow but I could feel a shift in his muscles.

"And what will we do up there, then?" The joint was about to burn his fingers; he stared at it, then tossed it into the temple and looked back up at me. He'd turned so the moon caught his face trying to settle itself.

I raised my eyebrows at him and smiled, wanting to be coy

but knowing it was all wrong on me.

"Clare." He frowned.

"Oh, for Christ's sake, Niall, stop treating me like an infant." I stood and began brushing the dust from the seat of my jeans but he didn't move.

I was flattered. It was the first uncertainty I'd seen on him and it felt pure, like I'd stirred something and he needed to examine it before he knew himself again.

"Is it proving yourself that you want to do?" he said. "It's not necessary."

"No. I want to."

He smiled gently. "And the truth is, I'm not altogether recovered. But I might well be in an hour or so."

A bitter moisture rose through my chest. I swung around headed up the hill. "Hell," I called over my shoulder, "I've got the whole night."

I wasn't sure he'd follow me but eventually he did.

There was no one in the castle. It was hollow and blind and the cold echo of the stones around us would have been lonely if it hadn't been for him. His first touch frightened me, coming as it did out of the black void. Then I remembered that it was not a void, but him, and I lay down. The ground was cold and heavy against my back.

It didn't take us long. He was ready no matter what he'd said. It hurt me and I don't think he'd expected that I'd never done it before. But afterwards, to his credit, he held me while I bled into the dank earth and managed not to cry.

Yes, kind, but he didn't remember me. I waited and waited this evening while he darted back and forth pulling pints and handing ashtrays. The place was filling up and I tried not to look like a kitten at the SPCA begging to be taken home.

Finally, as he passed along the bar again, he glanced at me and saw me watching. He gave me a brief sort of bemused smile. "And what can I get for you, darling?"

Then he paused and contemplated me. A ripple of memory passed over the thin pale pocks of his face. "I know you," he said.

Relief billowed up in me like smoke.

"Aye, of course." He smiled. His face is craggy and old-looking as ever although he must only be about twenty-five. His hair is still white-blond and rippled and halfway down his back; tonight it was tied in a horse-tail bundle. "Clare. From ... Canada, wasn't it? My apologies. Why don't you have a pint on me, so."

He pulled a quick Guinness and left it on the grille to rest. Then he bustled away toward someone who'd called his name. When he came back he finished the pint with a jerk and pushed it over the bar to me. I asked him for a tomato sandwich.

As I waited for him to return I looked around; I hadn't dared to before in case I missed catching his eye. Everything in the pub is in the same place: the tables by the windows looking down and out to the ocean, the benches in the corner for the musicians, the bar shiny and dark. The menu hasn't changed: vegetable soup, fish and chips, toasted sandwiches. Harp, Smithwick's, Guinness and Budweiser on the taps. The place was filling up, shouts and splashes and laughter getting thicker. A few men with guitar and fiddle cases shooed people away from the musician's corner and set themselves up.

Niall called something in Irish to the other barman, dropped his rag onto the counter and came around the bar.

He placed my plate squarely before me with a significant smile as though the sandwich were a talisman of great importance.

"So what would you be doing back in Aran, Clare?" He slid onto the stool next to me, his tail of hair slapping me gently before settling along his sinewy neck. I bit into the sandwich, pulled open the bread to look inside. The tomatoes were pale and flavourless.

"I'm here to see Gilly."

"Gilly? O yes, Gillian — she's your cousin, is she not?"

"That's right." I didn't know where to put my hands or my attention. I picked up the sandwich again and watched it, hoping it would do something. The voices of people who'd been here forever and people who'd come for the night were rising and ringing. His eyes were steady and I knew that my eyes were not.

"Will you be going over to see her mother, then?"

My stomach clutched. I put the sandwich down as it wasn't helping me. His face was calm and curious, just making conversation.

"Over where to see her mother?"

He raised his eyebrows and paused. "Don't you know?" I shook my head tersely. He hesitated again and then shrugged. "Well, it's no secret."

Niall pushed a wisp of his birch-blond hair behind his ears and stared straight ahead into the mirrors behind the bar. He always was a bit vain. He also never liked to look people in the eye unless he felt there was some weight to the exchange. "She's put Rosary in a rest home in Galway. They say she'll be back in a year or so, just needs some time to settle her nerves. She's a tough one, Rosary, she'll be all right."

He glanced at my face.

O Auntie. I wish I'd run right out of the pub then and down the hill to Gillian's house, I wish I'd broken down her door and tied her up and tortured her until she promised to get on the boat with me that minute and go and get you. But instead I swallowed and waited for him to say something else, for another heartful of his flinting voice.

"How's Gillian coming along, then?" he asked.

I picked up my sandwich again. "Shouldn't you know? She lives just around the hill."

"Aye, it's not far, but she's a bit private. When she came back from England I was married, and we haven't seen much of one another since then."

"Married?"

He grinned. His teeth still remind me of walls falling down. "Yes, I've got myself a wife now, Clary."

I laughed. I did. It wasn't that I thought he was joking exactly. It was more that I thought God was playing one of His tricks and I wanted to acknowledge it, more out of fear than anything else, not because it was funny.

I abandoned the sandwich. Even if I'd still been hungry it wasn't very good. His pack of Sweet Aftons was on the bar; I gestured to it and he held it out. I took one and he whipped out a lighter and lit it for me.

"Who's your wife?" I asked.

"No one you would have known. Her name's Grainne, but she likes to go by Grace, although I'm trying to talk her out of it. A nice Galway girl who came for a weekend and decided to stay. We've a baby on the way too. She'll be in later .... O she's here, she must've just arrived. There by the window, the long-haired one."

A heavy-faced young woman with big ornamental glasses and mouse-coloured hair thick as rain down to her backside stood over a table at the window and spoke down seriously to some girls, girls of about fourteen or fifteen, girls who could have been Gilly and me when I was last here. They laughed at her, waved their cigarettes toward her belly which was big under the elastic of her denim skirt but could have been naturally and not pregnantly round.

"When's the baby due?" I tried to make my lips do what lips are supposed to, but my teeth sunk into my cheek and I started. The taste of blood brought tears to my eyes. I rinsed my mouth with a sting of Guinness.

Grainne frowned at the girls but then smiled and ran her hand over the hair of one of the very blond ones. The girl moved her head away, then shifted back again and rested her temple against Grainne's hip. Grainne draped an arm, loose and white in its short blue sleeve, around the girl's shoulder.

"Not for seven months almost; we're just after finding out."

The sting passed.

I finished my Guinness with a couple of swallows. He got up, scooped the glass quickly, maybe to get me another, but I was afraid he might go and not come back. I laid a couple of fingers on his thin freckled wrist. "Are you happy?" I asked.

He leaned an elbow on the bar and contemplated me with strange gravity. "Couldn't be happier. And you, little Clare?"

"What?"

He glanced at my belly. "Are you happy?"

I paused with a shock. I tried to laugh again but it came out a cough.

"I should take that pint away from you," he said, "I'd not have given it if I'd known. And you're smoking, too."

I looked away from him toward the mirrors behind the bar. My hair was flat and frizzy all at once, that indeterminate almost-dark but almost-light colour that catches no one's attention. My face was pale; I couldn't remember the last time I'd put on any cream or a bit of lipstick. I looked puffy and bruisable, but I couldn't see anything that would give me away.

"I could just be fat for all you know."

He was looking at me in the mirror too; his eyes met mine and he touched my shoulder lightly with the back of his hand. "You've always been a bit fat, Clare, but there's nothing wrong with that. No, there's something about the shape and colour of you that makes it obvious."

It couldn't have been, but if you'd asked me right that moment I would have told you the baby kicked me. Maybe it was my own heart jarring in an odd place; maybe it was the tomatoes or the Guinness gone down wrong. But there was a thump in me like an animal testing the bars of its cage.

The father's not an issue, Auntie, some man I met at *Shooters* and went off with so I wouldn't have to do the boy who'd been buying me drinks all night. I don't even remember the man's name. And yes, all right, it did occur to me right that moment as Niall waited for me to say something that if I had to have a baby I would have liked it to be his. But then my mother wanted her baby to be God's, didn't she?

Behind me in the mirror the musicians had settled into their places, the fiddler and the guitarist and the bodhran player. I remembered the bodhran player. He's a funny man, youngish but wrinkled and brown because he often works on the boats, with a smooth-shaven head and a few silver-capped teeth.

The fiddler began to reel gently, the notes tumbling like puppies.

I glanced toward Grainne again where she stood by the girls' table near the heavy door that leads toward the ocean. *How strange,* I thought. After all those pretty tourist girls who scared me so with their skinny legs and their bell-like laughter, this is the woman who took him. I watched her for a moment, the solid smile on her wide face and the awkward movement of her feet shifting one to another. You once told me, Auntie, that no matter how it seems, pretty girls are no happier than the rest of us. Looking at Grainne, then back at Niall, and then to Grainne again, I almost believed you for the first time.

The door opened behind Grainne. Teffia Mulvaney, barefoot in a creamy dress too thin for Ireland, sliced a cold breeze through the room.

What do you remember of Teffia's face? When was the last time you saw her? Teffia has a face like a freckled kitten: pug nose and pointed valentine chin, wide raspberry lips under strawberry hair. Eyes the colour of clear tea. Skin pink-spotted cream. Grainne looked up and over and smiled but Teffia ignored her and swept to the benches where the fiddler fiddled and the guitar player and the bodhran player waited. Teffia slid onto the bench beside the fiddler and watched the bow smacking the strings.

They were all coming back to me now. The fiddler stocky and balding who stopped in the middle of thundering jigs to pull out a huge flapping handkerchief and honk his nose. The reedy guitarist with the taped-up sliding glasses. Could they really be the same men five years later? Doesn't anyone ever leave this island when people like you and Grainne and the lady at the B&B keep coming to stay? And there used to be a piano too; I remember that night when Teffia and her father danced for us someone was hammering on a piano; a woman maybe; I don't remember her face.

Teffia looked up toward the bar and saw Niall and me side by side.

I was suddenly conscious of my unwashed hair frizzy from the salt and wind; of my prickly calves and the way my denims, cut off at the knees, pinched in all the wrong places. Her cream-white dress was no more than a piece of half-transparent cotton with darts at the waist and an eyelet neck and hem. She looked at me — I'm sure it was me she was looking at — for a long thick time and then turned her eyes back to the fiddle, pinching her lips together.

The guitarist joined the fiddler and they slipped and rolled and slowed into *"Mo Ghille Mear"*. A strange choice for the beginning of a night at the pub; after a few notes my body began to tighten and turn in on itself. The others around me quieted a little.

Teffia stood up. She didn't move forward but stayed next to the fiddler. Her eyes were on me again but then she closed them. The pub hushed except for a few of the ignorant tourists.

Niall was still leaning on the bar. I glanced at him and then across to where Teffia's white face was still and filling up in the mirror. The slow low thrum of the bodhran began faint in my middle and spread out through my limbs to my scalp and the tips of my fingers.

'Se mo laoch, mo Gille Mear

Teffia sang.

Even the tourists were quiet now. I glanced at Niall again. His eyes were on Teffia in the mirror but then he looked at me. He reached down the bar for a napkin and took a ball-point pen out of his shirt pocket.

'Sé mo laoch, mo Gille Mear
'Sé mo Shaesar Gille Mear
Suan ná séan ní bhfuaireas féin
Ó chuaigh i gcéain mo Ghiolla Mear

He handed the napkin to me.

I read the words over and tried to imagine what they might mean. The song went on and on and the bodhran rose underneath it, pounded and pulled below the surface like a rip tide. Finally Niall took the napkin from my fingers, fold-ed it out and wrote next to the Irish words:

He's my hero my shining star
He's my Caesar my shining star
Sleep nor happiness I've not had
Since my shining star went far away

I looked up at Teffia again, her open lips and the sea of her red hair, and I saw around the closed slits of her eyes the forehead and temples and heavy cheekbones of her father Michael. The two of them, nose to nose, swinging with their arms wrapped like love around each other's waists, her hair flying out a river of strawberry gold. And those same clenched eyelids a breath away from mine as the stones tore at my back and the carcass of the *Plassy* loomed black above me in the dark.

I extended my hand and closed it around the damp tepid glass of my Guinness, swallowed the night air bubbling up my throat.

I wanted to ask Niall: where did the man go? But Teffia's song went on and on and he was watching her now. He, like everyone around us, had forgotten that anything but her had ever existed.

I touched my other hand to his, ready to say goodbye. His eyes turned down to me and they were sad, heavy and grey in the dull pub light and too old for someone as young as he must still be. I paused and tried to remember if his eyes had always been as old as this.

One night not long before I left Ireland, when we were standing at the top of that broken castle wall, his arms tight around me as though to prevent the wind from blowing me away, I looked up into his face and saw it wet and glowing with tears. I reached a hand up to touch the wetness and he smiled down at me. "Wind will do that," he said, and laughed.

Teffia's song was rising to a close; the crowd was murmuring glad grief. Niall leaned and asked into my ear, "Will you be staying a while, then?"

I turned my head and my forehead brushed his nose. He pulled back a little, to gain perspective I suppose. I couldn't decide whether the answer to his question was yes or no. So I shrugged and got to my feet.

I took the napkin with me. Grainne didn't look my way as I went out through the door. She, like everyone else, was beginning her applause.

Outside the air was cooling quickly and it was finally dark. The sea below the graveyard wasn't calling to me; it didn't know I was there. It was talking to itself, amused by some joke so private that even you — and you know that sea far better than I do — wouldn't understand. As I came down the hill, around the road toward the sounds of shouts and American pop at the other pub and back to where I am now, at my window at the B&B, I knew I wouldn't find you on Inisheer anywhere and I wouldn't run into Gilly by accident. I suppose in my mind I'd enjoyed the idea of giving her a good scare, walking up behind her at the shop or the whole-foods restaurant by the church and waiting to see what she'd do. But if she never goes out I suppose I have to go find her.

I've been sitting here by the window for a while now trying to calm myself enough to sleep.

It's just about closing time at the hotel now but if I dart out this minute I won't run into too many people on the road, and although I'm afraid at night it's not the night itself that scares me, but the people I might find in it. And I doubt Gilly's changed so much that she'd be asleep at two in the morning.

VI

Gilly's squat green house needs paint, Auntie. As I came down the castle road I knew which one was hers. The salt air is peeling the skin from it in bits like an old sunburn. Around it flowers and grass burst up through limestone cracks in a cloud of odours, sandalwood cinnamon jasmine — these smells don't belong here in the salt mist off the Atlantic.

What a vista from that road, even in the dark. You descend and the island stretches to the sea which stretches to Galway, and in front of you are little houses curled out toward the graveyard; they follow each other like the sheep who decide with one mind to move from one little stonewalled patch of green to the next one, who step over just the right dip in the barrier one after another.

When I knocked no one answered. The windows were dark and curtained. It would've been easy to believe no one lived there.

The door was locked. In places like Inisheer people open closed doors and step into houses and call hello without wondering what might be happening inside. *There are things happening,* I thought. But it was two in the morning, for Christ's sake. I pounded for a little while and the door moved under my fist, budging and springing back again.

One of the windows was half-open, surly like Gilly's eyes when I used to try to wake her in the morning. It was on the second floor — not really a floor but the attic I supposed — and set like a cyclops eye into the peak of the roof, but big and low and not altogether out of my reach. It was dark inside but I stood under the window and heard rustles of movement.

"Gilly, I know you're in there," I called. "It's me. It's Clare."

The rustles stopped. A murmur; one voice then another. The limp white curtains shuddered.

"Gilly, I'm not going away until you open the door."

I stared for a while. Nothing happened. In the faint distance the sea spat and roiled.

In gym class I was never much good at things like parallel bars or rope-climbing, but there was never anything at the top of the rope that I needed.

I crouched and sprang as high as I could with my arms outstretched. Under my fingers the sill crumbled and splintered a little; paint fell in grey-green flakes. Remembering what someone once told me about feet, not knees, I pushed and pulled myself up and stuck my head through the open window. Half of me fell into the house while the other half dangled outside.

The room was dim; the only milky light came from the moon through the white curtains and spilled across the bed. There was dust all over the floor and the walls were bare and grey in the dark. Salt air pushed through heavy spice incense and through something else like unwashed bodies licked clean by sea wind. A quilt was crumpled on the floor near the bed, the bed where Gillian was tangled in a mass of sheets and a curl-haired girl; small breasts and long limbs fell in all directions.

They pulled apart slowly and both turned, bored, half-awake, squinting toward my torso hanging through the window.

"O for fuck's sake," Gilly mumbled and reached toward the lamp.

She's the same, Auntie, all tiny bones and freckles, although her hair is cut into a short bush sticking out in licks all over, and she's even thinner; the grey-and-white sheet showed patches of barely-brown skin over bone. Her eyes were larger in her face, hollow and bloodshot, the pupils big. In the lamplight her freckles were pale, as though she hadn't seen sun in a long time. I could just see hints of Teffia: a little shock of strawberry curls lying over Gilly's breast; a creamy hand lying lazily at Gilly's waist.

In the time when I'd known them before I'd never caught them like this. Near the end, once I started to understand, I imagined them and so the sight wasn't altogether unfamiliar. I was jarred though, and before they'd untangled themselves completely I thought, hanging there, my legs waving like a bug's and the sill pressing a fissure into my abdomen: *No one has ever spent a whole night in bed with me. No one but Gilly.*

"Well, you should have known," I said.

I pulled myself through the rest of the window and almost fell on my head, but managed to somersault and land backwards on all fours like a crab, wrenching my arm. With a wince I straightened up onto my knees, brushed my hands together to sweep off the flattened threads of dust the floor left on them.

Next to the bed was a table with a dirty indigo-blue cloth; on it was a needle and a syringe with a drop of blood in it, and a red-leather-covered book. I leaned forward and inched toward the table. "Gilly. Is that the same Bible?" I reached a hand to the scarred leather cover.

"No, don't touch it, you nosy cunt." She turned her rigid

face to the ceiling and sighed, as though she was asking some-one up there for a favour and they were refusing to comply.

I wanted to be cool. I sat back on my heels and contemplated her for a moment. "I've got to be honest, Gilly; I'm insulted by your tone."

"Well, go away, then. I've nothing at all to say to you."

She'd been expecting me. She'd gotten my letter. She'd stopped returning me to sender. Or maybe when Teffia'd seen me at the pub she'd recognized me right away and had run off to fuck Gilly senseless the way a farmer brands a cow.

Gilly rolled over away from me and on top of Teffia's motionless frame to reach for something on the other side of the bed. Her naked skinny brown bum poked out of the sheets. She rolled back with a pack of Silk Cuts clutched in her hand and pulled the blankets up around her collarbones.

I let her have it. "How could you have put your mother away you ingrate cunt, don't you even care about your own fucking family, after all she did for you treating her like a worthless nutcase and look at yourself, you're the one who's lost your fucking marbles with your Bible and your goddamn junk" — at this point I picked up the syringe and needle from the table and flung them at her and then the red Bible too.

She just lay there, her eyes still only half-open and her mouth hinting at a smile. Teffia rose and curled around Gilly from behind, her face hovering just above Gilly's, her fingertips grazing Gilly's neck, her red curls showering around Gilly's head. Her eyebrows all twisted at me in something that looked like amusement. If there's one thing Teffia was always good at, it was making me feel like a fool.

I took a steadying breath and with a grimace I dropped into the dust on the floor and pulled myself away from them back toward the window, folded my legs into a lotus.

"Hello, Teffia Mulvaney," I said.

"Hello," said Teffia, sitting up slowly, pushing piles of tangled strawberry hair from her face. She wore a thin white slip torn clear down the middle and didn't bother to pull it over the freckled breast hanging out. "Who might you be?"

"My name is Clare Greening. You don't remember me."

She did remember me though; I could see it in the pale shadow of her sullen and unsurprised face.

Gilly picked up the Bible and the syringe from the bedclothes with careful, almost tender, hands. She placed the Bible back on the bedside table and laid the syringe delicately across it. "I don't remember you as the break-and-enter type, Clary Sage," she said.

"I'd like a cigarette if you don't mind, Gilly," I said extending my hand.

"Get your own cigarettes. A guest you are not."

Teffia pulled her legs from the sheets, draped them over Gilly to show me the black soles of her feet, and muttered something in Irish. Her mouth moved in her alabaster face like a snake coiling to strike. There are no snakes in Ireland, I reminded myself.

Gillian shrugged.

Teffia lay back and pulled a creamy dress, crumpled and dusty, from the floor on the other side of the bed and pulled it over her head. As she hoisted herself over Gilly and stood up the dress fell around her like foam on a Botticelli. Gilly watched as if seeing her for the first time, her eyes as open as they could be, her lips almost smiling. *Jesus,* I thought.

"Very fucking nice to see you again, Clare Greening," Teffia said. She looked at me for a moment as though she planned to step straight over my head, but she slid past me shadow-like, sat on the windowsill, swung her white legs around and dropped into the darkness.

I grinned. "Doesn't the door work?"

Gilly sat up, pulled the quilt from the floor and wrapped it around her shoulders. She ran a hand through the tufts of her shorn hair. "She doesn't like to be upstaged," she murmured, and lit a cigarette.

I was suddenly tired and cold. The curtains behind me waved half-heartedly against my back and I shivered, wondering if I should ask Gilly to give me one of the blankets from the bed. Instead I drew my knees up in my arms and waited for her to say something.

She sighed. Her black eyes fixed past me at the window. "What you want from me I don't know," she said. "I would have told you not to come if there'd been time, so."

"A cigarette is what I want from you. Are you going to give me a cigarette or not?"

She scooped the pack from the bed and threw it at me. It bounced off my chest and landed lightly on the floor beside me, stirring a few small tumbleclouds of dust. I raised my eyebrows and pulled out a cigarette.

"There was plenty of time," I said. I held out my hand for her lighter which she also threw, so hard that it clipped me on the temple. "OW! What's wrong with you? You had five years to tell me you'd lost your nerve."

She turned her eyes to the ceiling, blew a ring of smoke and then another.

She tried to teach me to do that once, that summer. We were lying on the bed in her little yellow room in the B&B with the window open and the sounds of shouts and fiddling coming from below. After a long hour of pursing my lips and twisting my tongue, finally sick with the steady stream of smoke, I gave up and said it looked pretentious anyway. She smirked at me and to escape I stuck my head out the window. Down below on the terrace of the pub next door a gang of about fifteen girls our age were dancing. The fiddler from the hotel, the balding man with the big handkerchiefs, was perched on the stone entranceway playing a merry reel for them and they were all laughing and stomping and twirling with ramrod backs, occasionally kicking one another unexpectedly in the shins and shrieking in apology. Around them a crowd of men and a few smiling mothers were clapping their hands and shouting words I didn't understand. I watched them for a while, expecting that Gilly would grow curious and stick her head out too, but when I finally pulled back inside she'd slipped out of the room and I hadn't even felt her go. She used to do that all the time. Disappear.

Now, fighting off shivers, I said, "Look at yourself." She was curled naked on the bed like a shrimp, blanket clutched around her, her Japanese skin turned almost as pale as mine. Hair greasy and sticking out all over. The smell of sweat masked by frankincense.

"You're one to fucking talk," she grumbled to the ceiling, "climbing in through windows where you're not wanted."

I sighed. "What was I supposed to do?" I demanded. "Wait until you came out to go to the post office? We had a deal. I'm ready."

"I don't have a notion what you're talking about. You are completely cracked. You can't just ... this is my *house*." She threw her hands in the air and the cigarette flew from her fingers. She fell across the covers to catch it as it came down and she hastily dropped it into something I couldn't see on the other side of the bed.

"Well, I can't afford the B&B, so I'm afraid you're going to have to accommodate me. Why don't you live there any more?"

"Surely you don't want to be hearing the story of my life at this hour in the morning." She squirmed around to rest her head on the pillow and pulled the quilt over her face.

My cigarette had burned down to the butt and was singeing my fingers. I pitched it at the window but it hit the sill and fell to the cracked hardwood floor, smoking. I slid over to it, picked it up and dropped it outside. I had an impulse: to lean out and see if it had fallen on anyone's head. We used to do that, wait at her window to drop things on the tourists, smoking butts or candy wrappers or stones we found in our shoes. I smiled thinking of it and glanced at her but she was still buried.

"Give me back my fags," she muttered into the blankets.

I pulled another one from the pack, lit it, tossed them and the lighter onto the mound of bedclothes. She pushed the blankets from her face and opened the pack, lit one and paused on one elbow, puffing for a minute. Her face was concentrated, her eyes on the floor, as though she were puzzling through a theorem. It reminded me of her Bible-reading face, the way she'd pause after reading aloud to me, ignoring my questions and staring at a point somewhere below or above us, her brows drawn together like she was trying to turn her gaze inside out.

"We promised," I said.

She slapped a hand down on the quilt, exasperated. "For the love of Christ, Clare. Things have changed."

I snorted, pulled my feet out from under me and wrapped

my arms around my knees again. "O yes, and for the better, I can see, now that you're shooting stuff into your arms. What kind of a life is this?"

"Fuck you."

"We swore on that same Bible." I pointed to it, lying on the table so smug and red.

Gillian dropped her cigarette on the other side of the bed again, rolled over and tossed the covers off. Naked she looks about nine years old; her breasts are so small you'd think they'd just begun. Only the patch of wiry hair between her legs and the roads of track marks up the inside of her arms make it clear she's not a little girl.

"What do you do here all day, Gillian?" I asked. "What's so important? Teffia Mulvaney?"

"Leave her out of this, you will." She stood and moved to the closet where she opened the door and collected a ratty pair of pyjamas, striped blue and grey, from the floor. As she pulled them on, her back to me, she said, "I make incense. For a shop in Galway. They give me oils and powders and I press them into cones and package them. That's what I've been doing with myself."

"That would account for the oppressive smell. And that's it? That's the essential service you can't abandon?"

She turned to face me. Her face battled itself like a sheet twisting in the wind. Finally she swallowed and said:

"There are those who need me."

A flash of Teffia's face in wailing orgasm, the buffet of salt breeze over the endless rocks on the other side of Inisheer. Teffia tearing away with her dress hanging open, retreating to a white speck on a white horizon.

"My memory of Teffia Mulvaney," I muttered, "is that

she's not the loving kind."

"You don't know a thing about her." She threw up her hands. "Jesus, why am I explaining myself to you? I can't believe we're having this conversation at all. If you want to stay the night, stay the night."

I stared at the burning end of my cigarette. "Why didn't we just do it right then and there? It would have saved us this whole discussion. I could have done without the last five years. Easily."

"But we didn't, did we, Clary?" Gilly closed the closet door and inspected her pale face in the mirror that hung on it; she ran a birdy hand through the hair that stuck out of her head. "We didn't do that. Why would that be, do you suppose?"

In the grey almost-light around her yellow bed in the B&B, her mouth so close to mine saying ... what I wanted her to say. That's one of the diseases we have, Auntie, all of us: you, me and Mumma. That disease that makes us wish for things so hard that we believe them. Maybe Gilly has it too but it didn't come from us. She doesn't have our blood.

"I always supposed," I said, "it was because you had things you wanted to do in the meantime." She pulled a pair of blue scuffed corduroy slippers, men's slippers too large for her, from under the end of the bed and stuck her little feet into them. "When was the last time you spoke to someone besides that red-haired whore? The people here say you never leave your house."

"Well, that is a simple misunderstanding. I am rarely going places where I meet other people, is all." Gilly sat on the bed with a heavy sigh and picked up the pack of Silk Cuts.

"I don't understand," I said, "how you can live with yourself."

The curtains retreated away from me and sank back against the window. A bird — what bird I don't know, a bird with a heavy satisfied voice — gave a single squawk in the distance. I turned my head to look and saw through the thin drapes that the sky had faded from black to charcoal grey.

Her hands in her lap were turning the pack of cigarettes around and around like a slow roulette in her fingers. Her shoulders were stooped and other than her hands nothing moved. For a moment I was ashamed. She looked so small and so tired.

She pulled out a cigarette and raised her eyes, black and resigned.

"It wasn't such a bad thing," she said.

Incredulity filled me to my eyeballs. I sat up on my heels and stared at her. I opened my mouth dramatically and waited for a long moment.

"What did you say? It wasn't such a bad thing? Is that what you said? There are worse things you could have done? And what would they have been?"

Gilly paused with her cigarette to her mouth, her thumb about to flint the lighter. Her eyes were huge round tobacco burns in her skinny face. She pulled the cigarette from her lips and said, "What she did to you. That was worse."

We looked at each other like that for a little while. The curtains stirred and brushed my neck as if fidgeting with sympathy.

The crush of stones against my back, the shadow of his head against the laughing stars, and me not able to make a sound.

"I didn't need saving," I said.

"You did."

"It was already over."

"Depends what you mean by 'it'."

"She didn't do it."

Gilly lit the cigarette then leaned her temple against one hand and closed her eyes, blowing a cloud. "It wasn't all her, certainly. I don't pretend I was entirely clear-headed. Which is all the more reason you can't possibly feel obligated."

"I'll keep my promise."

Gilly shuffled her feet in their big blue slippers, fell back on the bed and watched blue smoke float to the ceiling. "Well, I will not, Clary darling."

"I might have known."

"Yes, you might have." She stretched her feet toward me so I could see the cracked soles of the slippers, worn smooth and smudged with dirt. "You might have saved yourself the trip."

"I would have come in any case."

"What for?" She lowered her feet, still staring at the ceiling. "I'm sure you've a bottle of aspirin or a couple of razors at home."

"That isn't the point, Gilly. I can't believe you don't understand this at all."

"I wish you'd enlighten me, then."

A curtain billowed out and wrapped itself around my face. I struggled and slapped it away angrily. My chest was straining and then, once again, something kicked me where the baby was supposed to be. *Goddammit,* I thought, *shut up.*

It occurred to me then to tell her about the baby. It even occurred to me to tell her that until the baby happened I'd almost forgotten any promise we made. Or not forgotten but almost stopped believing. But speaking of babies would have made things worse, I'm sure. And what would've been the point? I can't really think of it as a baby anyway. One more corpse in the end.

I took a couple of deep breaths and listened to the sound of the sea. How the hell can it reach me all the way up here? I wondered. It's not fair. I wish I'd been born in a desert or an isolation tank.

"You and me ... " I paused. "Don't you have any consideration for the person you were then? I want to honour that." I stopped.

"Honour what?" I didn't answer. She sat up. "Honour me? Is that it, Clare? If it's honouring me you want to do, you'll go back home and forget all about this."

"It's not that."

"You want to be bound up with me for all eternity then, is that it?" Her hands flew wide again. "Because that's not how it works. In hell we won't get to be friends."

She flopped back onto the bed. There would have been silence if it hadn't been for the fucking sea.

"Is that it?" I asked.

"Is what it?" she muttered, the cigarette between her lips.

"You think you'll go to hell."

Her feet in their slippers stopped shuffling and her hand paused in the air. I watched it as it hung, suspended, the fingers frozen. Then her index curled slowly and began drawing small, steady circles as her hand moved toward her face. She plucked the cigarette delicately from her mouth. "Well, that might give me pause, yes, but not wanting to be dead is my most immediate concern." She sat up and threw her cigarette at the window; it sailed past my head in a perfect arc and disappeared outside. She stood up. "Clare, I'm very tired; I'd rather have this conversation in the morning if you think you can keep from killing yourself until then."

I didn't move. I clasped my knees to me and watched her where she stood, her face halfway smiling and halfway empty. *She doesn't believe me.*

"I'll wait until the moment, Gilly."

Her brows pulled together but this wasn't an inward gesture; all her impatience thundered out and at me like an assault.

"It isn't time yet," I said.

Gilly sighed again, crossed her twiggy arms across her flat chest and looked at me long and hard. Neither of us moved. Then she said,

"Do you know the story of Job?"

I frowned.

She tapped her slippered foot, one two three. "Job received his reward after enduring all the hardship God sent his way. No matter how shite his life was, he believed there was a reason for everything."

"But Gilly, there wasn't a reason." I sighed. "It was God playing a game."

Gilly shook her head and drummed the fingers of one hand against the bone above the other brown elbow. "He does not play games, Clary."

I didn't answer her. We waited.

Finally she shuffled her blue slippers toward the door. "You'll be needing a bed, then?" I didn't answer. She groaned almost inaudibly and then turned and vanished, clattering down the stairs. I sat unmoving and listened to her bang around in whatever was below. *This conversation is not over,* I thought, but I knew she'd be having no more of it tonight.

Auntie, you'd understand, wouldn't you? If you knew. The thing is it was her, it was her who said it. And she was right. The only way I could have gone on was to know it would end sometime soon. But I'll wait for the day; I won't break my promises, not me.

Maybe she thought that in the interim we'd do good things. Have lovers, see joy. Forget. Or something. She wanted me to go off and make her proud. That would have made her feel better. And what did I do? Talked to my therapist and learned to play the bodhran. And got myself pregnant.

And her? What's she been doing? Locked up in this house with one hand on the Bible and the other up Teffia Mulvaney's cunt. Making piles of smelly dust into little cones and selling it to people to burn in their houses. Sticking a needle into her arm. And then she talks to me about God.

If she thinks He's still watching over her now then nothing I say is going to make any difference.

VII

She put me to bed on the couch in the kitchen. It was full of lumps and springs and I couldn't sleep. I tossed and squirmed and listened to the ocean drone.

At four o'clock I got up, wearing a T-shirt and underwear, my fat legs all exposed. I wrapped my blanket around me, pulled my lighter and a crumpled cigarette that I'd stolen from Gilly out of the pocket of my souvenir-shop sweater, and took myself out to the front step. I closed the door, sat and put my back against it, lit the cigarette and tilted my head back to look at the sky. The moon was dull with the clouds and the beginnings of daylight; there were no stars at all.

I wished I'd made her tell me what the fuck she was doing putting you away. It didn't occur to me that maybe you were truly crazy, that you might have come at her with the spaghetti tongs or bitten one of the neighbours. It didn't occur to me because I knew — and I know now — it's not possible. I used to watch you, the way you'd stand over the stove stirring the tureen full of oatmeal and flipping breakfast fries of eggs and sausage and potatoes for twelve or fourteen people at a time, and you never even sighed. I'd come into the kitchen and your eyes would travel toward me like lighthouse beams making their steady half-circle and back again. "Good morning, Clary darling," you'd say, your voice cool and honey-thick. And I'd feel exactly what you meant: It's lovely to see you missy but I'm busy. You were clear and solid as quartz.

Some mornings, when Gilly wouldn't get out of bed and Mumma was doing God knows what, you and I would sit in that kitchen once the breakfast service was done, and if I wasn't too sick I'd eat your fry-up of eggs and rashers or white pudding or whatever else hadn't been finished off by the tourists. Sometimes you ate too, but other days you sat across from me, your hands steady on your teacup, and watched out the window. Watched nothing in particular; all we could see from the table was the blank blue-white of the sky. I thought I should make conversation but I'm not much good at that at the best of times, much less with someone I don't know. Occasionally though you'd say something. One day out of nowhere you turned from the window and your eyes on me were moderate and profound. You said,

"Niall is a good boy, Clare, but you're too young for all that."

I nodded and went on eating. You got up and started the dishes.

Some afternoons we'd sit in the front room, one at the piano and the other with a book because neither of us could sing and I couldn't play either, I'd just thrum as a sort of meditation which must have driven you mad. Sometimes when I was in there alone twiddling the keys you stuck your head in and offered to find me something to do. Subtle, that. But other times you stayed with me and let me sit there and press one note, then another, then several together, and you never asked what I was doing, you never suggested that I take lessons if I was so interested in making noise. That's what Gilly would have done, but she didn't learn that from you.

You could play though, and although the piano wasn't really in tune you made it sound good even if you were doing something like *"The Rose."* You had a way of holding the notes just a heartbeat longer than you were meant to, like waves poised at the crest before rolling over. Listening to you I wished that I could sing along but I wouldn't have dared.

That day I saw you and Teffia in the front room together, her singing in a low tremor and you smiling — I don't think I've ever felt so alone.

That last night when you told me you was going home in the morning, when you said that it was best for everyone and that you needed to think about what to do for you and Gilly, I felt that the only love left on earth had died. I'm sorry, Auntie. Maybe you thought it was my best chance; maybe you had hope for me. But there isn't any hope, there isn't anything. We've got poison in us.

You were my hope too.

I sat on the doorstep until the sun had mostly come up; it cast long tombstone shadows through the graveyard below and down into the sunken ruins of the temple. The island began to awaken. A man with a wheelbarrow trudged along the road below; he was far away but he must have seen me because he called out those words for Good Morning in Irish. Gilly taught them to me long ago but I don't remember them now. I was so astonished I didn't answer him. As he moved along I thought: *How can Gilly possibly live in this place?* If she wanted to shut herself up in a house and never see anyone, if she wanted the world to forget she exists then how can she live here without going mad?

I pulled the blanket around me and slipped back inside and up to her bedroom. She was still asleep; the dirty pale light of the morning fell through the curtains and across her bed, her cropped greasy hair going in all sorts of directions. The breath moved the freckles on the bones of her face.

Some of those nights that summer, in her bed in that yellow room, after we'd run out of things to whisper about if we'd been whispering that night at all, she fell asleep first and I watched her, her sheet of hair wrapping itself around her delicate neck, her lips sometimes moving silently and sometimes moving with Irish words which infuriated me; I wanted to shake her awake and shout *If you're going to tell secrets tell them in a language I know.* Some mornings I woke before she did and watched the colourless light on the skin of her shoulders. She seemed so perfect to me then, like a doll as long as her eyes were closed. Now she's different. In the early light her skin is ashen and tired.

She opened her eyes and said those Irish words for Good Morning.

I thought of smacking some colour in her cheeks, pulling at her hair until it reached her shoulders and lay in a river again, instead of sticking up so impudent and unruly. I thought of tearing off to the *Plassy* right then and hurling myself off just to show her I meant business.

But I didn't do any of those things. Instead I started to cry, which made me so furious that I ran back down the stairs, stripped off my clothes, pulled a blue sundress out of my bag and over my head, jammed my feet into my tennis shoes, and ran out of the house.

I ran up the hill away from her and away from the sea. I'm not a good runner, Auntie, as I'm too fat and I smoke too much so I soon had to stop and catch my breath, halfway up to the castle where the graveyard could protect me from the ocean. On the side of the hill halfway up and halfway down, graveyard below, castle above. The shadow of the hole in the ground which is the ruin of the temple of Saint Kevin. To go down, not up, to go down to the graves and sit on the broken walls with the dead people; it hit me so hard I dropped heavily onto the wall on the side of the road.

The walls are flat rocks piled in rows like sketches I've seen of cells, skin cells maybe. Flattened by one another, no visible gaps. But a stone has no nucleus, no membrane: it's all one thing. Divided, it doesn't change much; you can crack it open and it stays essentially the same. If you pile stones together they transmit nothing between them. All they are is a wall.

I sat and wiped the tears off my face and turned to look out over the walls and the beach and the sea. An old man passed, sidesaddle on a donkey, a basket on each of the donkey's sides. He nodded to me, said that word, moved along. A couple of cats chased, tumbled over one another, in haste and joy.

and when you're only halfway up you're neither up nor
down down down
down down down down down

Donkeys wandered down the hill, ignoring the black-and-white dog barking at their heels. The biggest donkey was at the front, the smallest at the back, two grey one brown one black. I never straightened out the difference between a donkey and a mule. I meant to ask Gilly once but there wasn't time.

Time: we had no idea then that nothing was urgent. We didn't know you'd send me home. I wanted to stay here forever. But you were about to take Gilly to England, you had to get away from all this and you had no money for me and her both.

Inching down the pier with Niall, Gilly walking slow behind us, as if we hoped the boat would leave without me. We didn't know a day or two days was all the same, this boat or the next one or no boat at all it didn't matter, none of it would change anything. You were sending me home to where people were waiting to try to make me forget, although I know the forgetting was not your idea.

When I was fifteen I'd lived by this ocean all my life. But not here. I didn't see why it would make a difference, one side of it or the other. Mumma did though. Mumma kept saying: We've never been there. But she'd never been anywhere and neither had I. I didn't know then why this place mattered and everywhere else was so many colours splashed in an atlas.

Mumma made me so many promises, Auntie. From the earliest time I can remember — the time in that house where it was always dark, when we never went outside and I never saw anyone but that man she called my father — she was always telling me the things we'd do someday. Someday we'd be able to go outside, she said, but it wasn't true — once I got to be outside she'd been taken away and there was no *we* any more. Someday we'd be a real family, she told me on those weekends she came to see me, a real family with a house and some dogs and a father. But I knew even then it wasn't going to happen. Someday we'd be with God, she said, together we'd be with God. I know now there isn't any God, but even if there is Mumma isn't with Him, and I probably won't be either.

The only promise she ever kept was that she'd bring me here to see you. Maybe she knew that it was the most important one. Looking out over the ocean she'd say, "We'll go there someday. That's where Rosary is." In those years after she died and you sent me home, I'd sometimes face east on the water and I'd look out toward where I believed Ireland was. I'd think: *That's where Rosary and Gilly are.* Sometimes I'd think of Niall too. But not Teffia. Almost never her.

But now — I looked down toward the beach and saw Teffia Mulvaney's red hair against the water.

She was sitting far away on the sand, just a copper-topped smudge, still in that dirty cream-coloured eyelet dress. I wondered if she'd been home, wondered where her home is. I never did see her house, never saw where she and her father did the things a family does. Thinking this I almost laughed aloud and I wasn't even ashamed of finding it funny.

I stood ready to go somewhere else but Teffia's head turned. She saw me despite the distance, knew that it was me, even though I have no red hair or white dress to set me apart from the rest of the world. Her arm, the underside almost the same colour as the beach and the sky — pale blue-white — rose and gestured.

I hesitated a moment, stood halfway up and halfway down, neither up nor down. And so was she, her arm still waiting in the air.

I picked my way down amongst the stones, kicked off my tennis shoes when I got to the sand. When I sank into the beach beside her she said, "I'm remembering you now."

Teffia's hair a strawberry cloud around her freckled face, cheekbones pink from the sun but not newly so. Feet bare and black on the bottoms and no shoes around. I wondered: does she cultivate that Maid of the Limberlost thing, the tangles and the dirty white dresses too cold for this place and the disregard for shoes and sweaters and umbrellas in the rain?

"Why, do you suppose," Teffia said slowly (her voice rough and clear and heavy and sweet altogether), "Gilly never told me you were coming?"

Teffia's bare legs, slender and soft and strong, unshaven of their down which was visible only because of a transparent copper catch of the light. Bare to the thighs where she'd hitched up her dress. Bent at the knee, feet deep in the sand at the heels, square toes with broken toenails poking out. Her dress falling away at the pink cream freckled shoulders.

"Do you believe," Teffia asked, putting her elbows on her knees and leaning toward me, "it's because she didn't want me to know? Or do you believe" — and she pulled away just as suddenly and lay back into the sand, pushed her heels and splayed like a snow angel, her eyes on me — "do you think it's because it didn't matter?"

Her body wide open as a jug with no lid. Her eyes unblinking tea brown. Like that day on the rocks on the other side when she pulled my hand up between her thighs without the bother of preamble.

I wanted to ask her to sing a song. I wanted to make some sort of use of a body so convenient and idle.

Children played further down the beach near the airstrip. I was shivering in my blue sundress, wishing I'd brought that black cardigan with me, but she was as comfortable in the cold sand as a cat in a patch of sun. Her face half-smiling as though she couldn't wait to see what I'd do next.

She hadn't looked at me much in those days. When she and Gilly and I wandered about, smoking cigarettes and drinking Guinness-in-disguise and getting wet and sandy and cranky, she spoke only to Gilly and only in that language

I didn't understand. It didn't feel like she couldn't see me though. It felt like she was willing me invisible.

I pulled my sundress overhead.

One of her strawberry eyebrows flickered and then sank back. She turned her head in the sand to give a slow glance toward the airstrip, toward the end of the beach where the gang of little children were waving their pails and dipping their feet. No one else was around. Auntie, what keeps the people of this island so busy that they have no time to notice the things going on all over the rocks and the sand and the ocean? No time or no strength.

I stood and walked to the edge of the waves, leaving her where she lay impressing an angel into the beach. I could see boats far out, one rapidly approaching until I made out the words *Aran Flyer* on the side. I imagined the pug-faced boathand looking my way and seeing my naked bobbing breasts with a distant jiggle of memory.

Clammy sand and freezing salt foam broke on me as I lay down near the edge of the tide.

The sky disappeared as the water chased over me, then returned as the wave receded. Seagulls were circling, laughing. *Fuck off,* I thought; *what do you know.* Covered with the sea I could be numb but when it pulled away my skin rose in gooseflesh, every tiny hair standing and crying out in pain. If it hadn't been for the rasping in my throat I wouldn't have known my tears from the seawater.

My mother's pale dress soaked in surf, darkening from eglantine to a watery rose, her hair tentacles of golden kelp.

The sand shifted with footsteps. Thinking of Teffia I raised my head out of the water and tilted it back to see the beach upside down, the sand turned to sky and the sky to sand, all white and blue and shimmering the cold day back and forth.

Teffia was gone. Gillian stood next to my shoulder, wearing shorts so high I could see pubic hair spill out the edges. A black bikini halter showed every pointy rib, the body of a child in one of those television ads meant to persuade fat people like me to give money to children turned to bone by famine. Track marks silver on the insides of her elbows. The water skittered lacy around her ankles. My head sank back into the foam.

"Would you be going stark bleeding mad?"

I barely heard her through the waves in my ears. I sat up and my hair stiffened with salt.

"The sea is not a fucking spa," Gilly said. "Is it pneumonia you're after?"

I was trying to catch the sobs in my chest. I wrapped over myself and curled my frigid feet the way a yoga teacher once taught me: point, flex, point, flex, tighten tighten tighten and then ... relax.

Slowly the heaving subsided. I stared down between my knees at the curdled surface of the water skittering with little rushes of foam, splashed my face and rubbed my eyes. This struck the sadness down and I giggled. I looked up to Gilly's bemused face and said, "Trying to wash tears with sea salt. My life has been an exercise in futile gestures."

She rolled her eyes and looked away down the beach toward the airstrip. I wondered which direction Teffia had run off in. "Try not to make a melodrama of everything," Gilly said absently. A wave hit my chest and washed over her knees.

"I beg your pardon? You're one to talk."

She frowned at me and looked up to the white sky, shivering. I turned my face up too. In patches the clouds were spreading, making room for a deep empty blue.

"I saw you through the window," she said, "down here with her. I wondered if you might be going to drown yourself. If you were, though, you picked a crap way to do it."

I put my head on the wet sand again and let a wave pass over my face; I choked and sat up; a whip of kelp lashed me across the eyes. Peeling it away I looked out across the grey ocean toward Galway. Gulls circled, shrieking. I wondered if they're like carrion crows or hawks, if they sense when people are dying, and wait for them.

I got to my feet. The ocean had seemed so greedy, so desperate, but as I began to walk out toward Galway it changed its mind. When the water reached my ribs a crest of foam knocked me down and pushed me back toward shore; I surfaced and opened my eyes and Gillian was still standing up to her ankles in surf, watching me. Seaweed and the transparent veined bodies of jellyfish fluttered past; one pulsing globe slapped my hand and I pulled away in panic.

We never knew if Mumma died right away, broken on the stones, or if her unconscious body knew about the salt and the living creatures that kept her company until she was gone. They didn't let me see her body afterwards, but I imagine it all the time, the dye in her pink dress running into magenta and white marbling, sheets of weed spilling around her swollen grey face, her divinity swallowed and washed away.

The waves kept trying to toss me back to Gilly. *It isn't time yet,* I thought, floating. I pushed my feet against the sharp shells buried in the bottom, propelled myself back through the thick tremors and wisps of weed, crawled out onto the beach.

I lay down on the sand spluttering and shivering.

She stood over me with her black eyebrows drawn together. Against the sky she looked like the shadow of death, all bones and patience. Then she picked up my blue sundress and tossed it on top of me where it could absorb the cold dirty salt.

"Cover yourself, for Christ's sake," she said. "I'll go put on the kettle."

She turned her back and headed away up the hill to the road.

None of the children further down the beach seemed to see me as I sat drenched and naked, clutching a blue sundress to the pricks of my shrunken nipples. The day was pale all around me and I stayed alone on the sand for a while, heavy and dead as if I really had drowned.

It wasn't at all like that night we ran out onto the sand together bare to the sunrise, jumping to keep warm and laughing with the aftermath of weed and cider and exhilaration. That night she waited for me as I gathered up all the scraps of my clothes, and we ran back to the B&B together along the pier road, the asphalt under our feet already beginning to warm in the first inklings of the early sun.

VIII

I went to the B&B this morning to get the rest of my things and to tell the lady I wouldn't be back. She nodded, wrote me a bill, took my money and asked no questions. Much the way you would have, Auntie. Perhaps that's what you learn if you spend your days feeding and housing strangers; all these stories passing through your home cease to be novel or interesting. She handed me the receipt, said, "Good luck to you, dear," and headed back to the interior of the house with a sponge in her hand.

I wanted to look around some more, see the rooms she lives in, the rooms I lived in for that summer: the kitchen, the family bedrooms. It seemed presumptuous so I didn't ask. I did, after I'd packed up my little bag, go into the front room, which was always shared with the guests. The piano is still there; I think it's the same piano. I stood next to it for a while and I watched out the window which looks over the pier where the children congregate around the chipper and the boats come to and fro. It was a sunny day today and the gulls seemed happy, circling and shouting. Families lolled on the beach. Some were in bathing suits and splashed in the water although it was no more than fifteen degrees; some rolled their pant legs and walked along the surf; some sat on the sand with sweaters and books, bare toes buried.

I turned to the piano and thought about tonic chords, wondered how one would go about making one.

I left the B&B and walked up to the shop to buy Gilly some groceries. I'd looked around the kitchen before I left and found it bare; I suppose from the looks of Gilly it's possible she never eats. I don't know how to cook much but I can make a sandwich and boil an egg.

The shop is still small and the cans and boxes look orderly but slightly confused on the shelves, as though they're in the right places but aren't sure how they got there and keep looking around in amazement. I brought some bread and juice and apples and cheese up to the counter and had to wait behind a family of tourists. Their conversation sounded like German maybe; it wasn't Irish because the man at the counter didn't understand them. There were a mother and a father and five boys; the oldest was about fourteen and handsome with big chocolate eyes and a minkpelt of dark hair. He held the youngest in his arms, a baby wrapped in a thin blue blanket. A gaggle of teenage girls came in looking for crisps and *Ballygowan,* and as they swarmed around us at the counter a couple of them peered into the baby's face and touched his pomegranate cheeks with long freckled fingers. They looked up at his teenage brother and smiled and he averted his eyes. When he and his family gathered their purchases and trickled outside the girls looked at each other, giggled and whispered in Irish.

The man who rang in my groceries was huge-bellied and old with tufts of yellow-white hair, and I asked him for tampons to see him mutter and blush no. Good thing, too, because I have no use for them and wouldn't have wanted to pay. You couldn't buy anything but pads last time I was here — sanitary towels Gilly called them — and I just wanted to check how much things had changed. The time I asked Gilly why I couldn't find Tampax she said, "Because they still hope nice Catholic girls wouldn't know what to do with them, and good married ladies would be too busy pregnant to ever have a period. Have to keep up the population of the Gaeltacht, you see."

It made me think of you, Auntie, who never had a baby, even the one you started.

As I walked back down toward Gilly's house someone was coming up the road. It was the pug-faced boat-hand who once saw my boobs on the boat. He stamped along toward me as though the earth was too solid under his feet, his flat face angled toward the ground a few feet in front of him. He turned in at Gilly's door and knocked.

Gilly came out just as I arrived on the doorstep and the boat-hand gave her a package wrapped in brown paper. She took it without a word and handed him more money than I expect you would pay for a few ounces of powdered incense. The boat-hand turned and left without looking at me as I closed the door behind him.

I didn't ask Gilly what the package was. I put my groceries down on the table and put the kettle on. She took the bundle up to her room and didn't come down for half an hour or so. When she did her eyelids were heavy and the thin flesh of her face serene.

I told her about the lumps in the couch, so she hauled a mattress into the little sitting room off the kitchen while I made cheese sandwiches and tea. When she was done with the bed she came obligingly to the table, but she took one bite of her sandwich and then just sat with her mug of tea warming her hands, like you used to in the mornings, Auntie. She watched out the window where the day was trundling along with its donkeys and wagons and pickup trucks. I imagined the little buildings around us full of housewives with TVs tuned to the Irish soap operas, and little children reciting their multiplication tables in strange impenetrable numbers, and teenagers from Dublin doing conjugations, if verbs in Irish conjugate at all. I thought of asking Gilly but I had a feeling she wouldn't know what I meant, and besides she didn't look like she wanted to be asked anything. She didn't look like she wanted me at all. She just kept staring straight ahead out the window as if imagining herself somewhere else. Finally I dumped the crusts of my sandwich into the trash and stepped out the door without saying a word, leaving her to notice or not that I was no longer there.

I could feel the *Plassy* far to the east calling me; I even believed, as it was a clear day, that I could see it looming off in the distance, a shadow of rust against the faint sky. I turned when I reached the road and was soon picking my way through the big smooth stones of the eastern beach. Flat smooth stones; wet crags rife with barnacles like a cheesegrater; pillars, obelisks. Occasional tumbles of hairy wet weeds, dark and grasping.

The first time Gilly took me out here we came from the other side, having been on the western beach near St. Enda's well, looking out to where I'd come from. The beach was the same out that way, all rock and crags, slippery with deceptive hidden teeth. I'd wanted to take off my shoes that day but I was afraid of sharp surprises. It was sunny I remember, sunny and hot, the hottest I'd ever known it to be in Ireland. The *Plassy* far away was a hulk of dissolving rust leaning away from the sea. The outline of a big yellow sign on the ship's side said DO NOT ENTER. Gilly didn't wait for me; she was nimble and moved easily among the slippery rocks while I had to watch my feet and test each step. As I approached the boat from the inner beach, a thousand stones between me and the sea, Gilly so far ahead that from my perspective she seemed pressed against the rust-brown side of the *Plassy*'s hull, I looked up and toward the water over the white and grey ripples of rock bright in the sun, and I saw:

A black-haired squat man with a black thick moustache, heavyset, perched on a rock in the middle of the expanse of beach. I couldn't see his eyes; he was too far away and the bareness of the light hurt my eyes. He wore blue denims and a cheap-looking short-sleeved blue shirt with buttons. As I passed him far up the beach he turned his head to look, although I was too far away for him to speak to me.

I began to see something near his feet. A pale strawberry rippled head, and bare white shoulders. She sat in a recess, perhaps a pool. Her face was in profile. It was impossible to say at that distance if she was pretty but she looked young, as young as me, and he looked old, much older than my mother. I imagined pale freckles on her pale skin. I imagined she had no clothes. He sat with his feet planted apart on the rocks near her head.

Gilly hadn't looked at them as far as I noticed. When I caught up to her she didn't say a word and I couldn't bring myself to ask. But how could she have missed such a black head and such an orange one against the stark hot white-blue of sky and sea, the white-grey of stone?

Picking my way through the stones to the boat again today I found myself looking over my shoulder. I don't know where he is, Michael Mulvaney; he could be anywhere. Maybe I should ask Teffia.

The *Plassy* is a great flaking scar of a dead ship tipping itself toward the ocean. It doesn't seem any more rotten than it was five years ago. I asked Gilly about it that first day I saw it, what it was and what it was doing there, but she just shrugged. "It's an old boat," she said and tripped on ahead, leaving me to struggle with my heavy feet. Later Niall and I came out there together in the early evening and he told me; Niall seemed to always know the things I wanted to know. It was wrecked in the sixties he said, and then thrown up on the shore. Nobody had died. That was comforting to me, that nobody had died.

When Gilly and I had sat on that beach watching the boat in the blank heat of that single sunny day I'd only been there a few days and I didn't know how to talk to her, worried that whatever I said would be wrong. (I hoped that feeling would go away sometime but of course it never did.) So we sat in silence listening to the murmur of the waves grown listless in the unfamiliar warmth.

Out of nowhere Gilly had said, "It's all so pitiful. When you think about it."

I'd rubbed a hand across one of my bare shoulders and wished I'd brought some sun cream, but who would have thought of such a thing in Ireland? "What is?"

She tilted her face back toward the blazing sky. "What does it matter? What christly difference does it make, anything we do? On this goddamn rock in the ocean." She sighed. "Sooner or later the world's going to burn up or burn out or explode or the Judgment Day will come, and nothing I'm after doing will change that." She kicked one of her bare brown feet through a patch of dry sand.

I'd paused for a moment, wondering where this thought had come from and whether she was expecting an answer, whether she realized at all that she was talking to me. When she didn't continue I said, "But if the Judgment Day comes, everything you've done will matter."

Gilly laughed shortly and shook her head at the sun. "Only to me," she said. "Only to me."

And to me. It already matters to me.

The next time we went out there together was the night Mumma died.

When I reached the boat today I sat on the rocks for a while and looked at it. I didn't go inside. The big rusted signs say *DANGER* and *SEACHAIN* — when I first saw them I wondered what a seachain was, and thought it sounded very poetic until Gilly told me it's Irish for 'beware'. Today I sat alone and watched the boat and waited for it to say something, do something. It leaned, tired and indifferent. I thought of walking around to the other side, to the face that looks out over the water. But I didn't.

I wished that I had voices to listen to. I wished that someone would speak to me the way the angels used to talk to Mumma. It must ease the loneliness to have a head full of instructions, full of messengers sent especially for you. But my mind was empty and buzzing and the only voices came from the seagulls, and the waves, which struggled to touch the *Plassy* but fell short over and over and broke on the rocks far out with disappointed cries.

And as I sat unmoving I could have sworn that for a single and brief second I saw a spot of pink and gold high up on the deck against the sky. I froze rigid on my seat of stone and blinked my eyes but the spot was gone. I rose slowly to my feet, and strained to see what it could have been: a tourist ignoring the warnings of the *seachain,* a big foreign bird straying ludicrously far from home, a rose-coloured cloud who'd slept late and missed the sunrise. But there was nothing. A trick of the light no doubt, or of the mind.

It was several minutes before I could move again and when I did I took myself quickly back along the stone beach toward Gilly's house, my heart hammering, not once looking over my shoulder at the ghost boat behind me.

IX

The days are sandy and cold here. It hasn't rained but the sky has been a cool marble-grey; it's impossible to tell where the sea ends. At night the stars don't come out.

I've been having that dream again; I had it last night. The one where I climb down to a river and when I get there I have something in my hand that I didn't have before. This time I looked at the thing — I don't know what it was, I don't even know if I could see it while I was dreaming. I looked at it though, straight at it, and then I heaved it out and over the river. It didn't fall in the water. It flew on outward, kept going and going until it disappeared. It might have fallen once it was out of my sight but I suppose in a dream things only happen if you see them happen. Once it was gone I stood waiting, but then the baby kicked me and I woke up.

Gilly's house is dreary, Auntie. I don't like it that she lives here. The walls are bare and dirty; all the furniture is broken. There's no television, no stereo, no books except the red Bible. On the first floor is the kitchen, a small washroom with a dirty toilet, and a little alcove where she's made me a bed; her room is in the peak of the roof with a closet-sized workshop where she keeps her oils and powders and jars. Even with the windows open the smell of incongruous plants hangs fog-like over everything; it nauseates me.

Each morning I haul myself blurr-eyed to the kitchen and usually Gilly's alone at the table with a mug of tea, staring at the wall. I make a cup too, and then we sit unspeaking across from one another, sipping, until we think of something to say. "So what is it you've been doing all this time, then," was the opener from her this morning; it was so dull it was barely a question at all.

Nothing, that's what. You didn't get my letters so you wouldn't know either. I worked in a pizza parlour and spent a lot of time talking to the counselor at my old high school. I'd seen him every week when I was a student and we'd gotten in the habit of it, so when I got back he agreed to see me again. Mr. Pike was his name. He was rather dignified and handsome in a nondescript, greying sort of way, like one of those second-rate older movie stars who all look kind of the same. He'd say things like: "Don't you feel angry, Clare?" And I'd say, "Yes, Mr. Pike, I feel angry." "And what do you feel angry about, Clare?" "I don't know, Mr. Pike, what do you think I should feel angry about today?" Then he'd close his eyes, give a short tense sigh and lean back in his chair and wait until he got tired of me smiling at him. Or he'd ask: "Do you miss your mother, Clare?" And I'd say, "No, Mr. Pike, I don't miss my mother." "Why not, Clare?"

He was very patient; I admired him. He would always fold his hands exactly in the center of his desk, his back bookbinding-straight. But what was I supposed to say? He wouldn't have believed the truth if I'd told it to him. He didn't have the slightest idea what he was getting himself into. I told him that sometimes. "Mr. Pike, you don't have the slightest idea what you're getting into." And sometimes he sighed and said, "I'm not getting into anything, Clare."

When I got pregnant the Cassatts said I mustn't worry, they'd help me raise the baby or even adopt it if I wanted them to. That's why I couldn't tell them when I left; I had to pack in secret and sneak out of the house in the wee hours before they were awake. They would have tried to stop me. It's not that I'm not grateful, to you for hoping for a life for me, to the the Cassatts for trying to give it. I sometimes wish I were the kind of person who could've moved on and risen above. But I can't rise above anything. None of us can, although I would have believed you could.

So when she asked me this morning I didn't answer. I said, "We swore on that same fucking Bible, Gilly."

"I'll rip it to pieces if it'll make you go home," she replied, her eyes still blank on the wall, her mug loose and cooling in her hands. I didn't say anything. "Think of the baby, then," she said.

She guessed about the baby one night when she tossed me a t-shirt to sleep in and watched me undress. The biggest shirt she owns and I couldn't pull it over the little bulge in my belly. It keeps kicking me all the time, although I don't know how it's possible yet, and I want to punch it down like those loaves of unbaked bread you used to smack into submission. *It's your fault,* I tell it silently. *Otherwise I might have forgotten.*

Every second morning Gilly takes out a soup pot and throws a ham bone and an onion and a potato and a carrot into it, fills it with water and sets it on the stove. Then she turns the pot on. She picks up her half-warm mug and I follow her upstairs, to sit with a book on her bed and smoke her cigarettes and watch her through the workshop door while she putters around. For half the day every day she presses scented dust into little cones, pours oils around. Rose sandalwood patchouli jasmine. Clary sage. She sets fire to things, heats them on her little Bunsen burner, cools them, stirs them. It all seems unnecessary to me, and a little offensive. Things should smell the way they smell; they shouldn't smell like places far away. But she always lets me sit there and I don't leave. I watch her pack up the little cones and once a week she gives them to the boat-hand when he comes by with her bundle of whatever.

At lunchtime we go back to the kitchen and sit at the table and eat some of her soup. It tastes of bones and onions and starch. Soup and toast seem to be all she eats, and not much of them. If I knew how to cook I'd make her something else, roast her a chicken or bake a lasagna. With all the smells around here you'd think she'd know something about flavour. But she doesn't seem to care.

Today we sat silently until I said, "Well, why don't you tell me about England?"

She raised her eyes to mine. It was the first time all day she'd looked me in the eyes. She put a couple more spoonfuls of soup to her mouth, and then put the spoon down.

"Mam wanted to get away. She thought it was better for me. We stayed four years and I'd had enough."

She pushed the soup bowl away from her and stood to put the kettle on again.

"So you made her come back here." She didn't answer. "And then you sent her off." It was as if I wasn't there. "I don't understand, Gillian, how you can care so little about your own fucking mother."

"You're one to talk," she said evenly. "Have you cried for her once, you frozen twat?"

It took me a moment to realize she wasn't talking about you. Then I said, "Yes. Yes, I have."

But she'd already disappeared up the stairs, to get her Bible. I watched the empty space across the table from me until she came back and filled it. She turned her chair backwards and threw her legs around it and settled the King James open on the tabletop. That's what she does every afternoon, Auntie, for hours and hours. How could you have let this go on?

I watched for a few minutes as she read, her lips moving slightly. I knew she wouldn't speak again unless I made her.

"Why don't you read me something," I said. "Like you used to." She looked up, her black eyebrows drawn together. "Come on."

"What good would it be doing you?"

"I like the sound of it."

Her eyes clenched. "Have you nothing else to do, so? A book to read, a boy to visit, a plane to catch?"

"Just read me a verse. Something you like."

She sighed. "It's not a question of like or don't like. You wouldn't understand anything."

I look at that Bible sometimes and think about taking it down to the beach to burn it, to throw it into the sea. I haven't yet. The waves would just toss it back to me. The sea kills things but it doesn't keep them; it's the same where I come from. That's one of the reasons this place could have been mine. The other reason is that I felt right with them, in the haze of liquor and weed, in the dark. I felt that there was room for me.

There was that one night near the end of that first summer when Gilly fell from the pier. We'd been at the pub long after closing, and then Gilly and Niall and Teffia and me, and a bunch of those boys who always hovered around, had wandered down to see if we could spot sea otters. (I don't know who suggested otters; it might have been me; I swore to them that I'd seen one when we'd come over on the boat, although I didn't know how to tell an otter from a seal when they were in the water.) Gilly'd been the drunkest I'd ever seen her, staggering and occasionally sick; on the short walk from the hotel Teffia had to drop behind with her several times to hold the hair off her face and to prop her up and keep her moving. Then we all forgot about Gilly for a moment as we sat on the concrete sides of the pier lighting joints and laughing. At one point I said something — I don't remember what — and Teffia turned her eyes on me. She was giggling and we locked our gazes together for a conspiratorial heartbeat. Niall's arm tightened around my shoulder.

When we looked up Gilly was standing on the end beyond the moored boats, one leg stuck out like the needle of a compass and her hands wide and fibrillating. "Otters!" she shouted.

Teffia and I leapt to our feet and dashed toward her, the boys not far behind, just to see her topple and shriek and disappear with an almost inaudible splash. Teffia was about to go over after her but I grabbed her around the waist and Niall began shouting orders until we organized ourselves. Niall and another boy took Teffia's ankles and lowered her over the side until she could clutch Gilly under the arms. I wanted to help but Teffia managed to hold on to her until the boys had pulled both of them back up to the pier. Gilly, slick with salt and dissolved litter, lay laughing on the ground, shouting "Otters!" again and again until Teffia burst into tears and kicked her in the ribs. I don't think Gilly even felt it; she just lay there laughing.

Did you ever fear that your daughter who you brought here from halfway around the world might one night go someplace even further and never come home? Because she almost did, you know, more than once. And she's still trying to, no matter what she says. Filling her veins with poison so she can be just like us. Haven't you been paying attention?

Answer me, Auntie. I know you can hear me no matter what walls are making you think you're safe.

At night Gilly goes into her room, to shoot up that stuff the boat-hand brings her I suppose. Sometimes Teffia comes and I try not to listen. Like you did I'm sure. But some nights Gilly goes away and doesn't come back until morning.

X

Tonight at the pub I sipped at a pint at the bar while Niall ran about with his ponytail flapping. His forehead was tense. Grainne was moving heavily between the tables gathering empty soup bowls and smiling patiently at orders, her long thick frizz of hair occasionally dipping into someone's pint. When she slipped past me and behind the bar Niall barked something Irish at her and slammed the flat of his hand down. Then he turned and skittered away. She frowned at his back and reached for one of the taps.

The floor was rumbling with shouts and the slapping of knees and the gallop of the musicians on their strings and skins. I turned my chair around to watch them. They'd rolled a piano in from somewhere but I didn't recognize the man playing; he was young, not much more than a boy, tall and weedy with thick black hair and big hands. He sat with his back to me; I couldn't see his face. There was another man on a whistle and I didn't know him either. They were cheerful, calling to each other in Irish over one another's heads, drumming their feet and grinning through the cigarettes hanging from the corners of their mouths.

I listened to the thrum brute pulse of guitar punctuation and the shower of the piano and I wanted a storm outside. A storm that would pound on the door until it broke open, a storm that would rip at the floor with rain.

When Teffia came in late and swept to the benches, Niall gave the bar a vicious wipe and with a nod to Padraic the fat freckled barman dropped into the high bar chair next to me.

"Hello, Clare," he said.

I didn't know what to say so I just nodded. I glanced over my shoulder at Grainne who was behind the bar again grabbing things and pushing them around. She didn't look up at me. She didn't look up at either of us. Niall was staring straight ahead to where Teffia stood silent with her eyes closed in her filmy bit of white cotton with no shoes on her feet.

"Doesn't she ever get cold?" I asked.

Niall glanced at me and gave a short laugh. "Teffie has enough heat in her to warm us all through many winters."

A flash of the possibility of his boney hand in the warm purse between her legs pulled my groin up through my stomach.

The fiddle rolled into *"My Match It is Made"*. It was a merry tune this time, and Teffia's voice isn't really suited to merriment; as she began she cracked occasionally between one note and the next as though it couldn't keep up.

The crowd wasn't silent tonight. They quieted a little as Teffia began singing but then rose to a roar again, in no mood to watch someone make noise when they were capable of making it themselves.

My match it was made here last night
To a girl I neither love nor like
So I'll take my own advice and I'll leave her behind
And I'll wander the wild world over

After a moment of polite concentration Niall swung his legs around the side of his chair and propped his elbows on his knees, his hands dangling between his thighs, his face not far from mine. "Do you sing yourself, Clare?"

I shook my head. "You?"

"I do not. I envy her that."

"Can you play anything?"

He reached for my pint and took a quick, surreptitious gulp, then wiped the back of his hand across his mouth. "They tried to teach me the bodhran when I was a lad. I've no rhythm in me at all, I'm afraid."

"I've been learning the bodhran," I said, taking my glass from his hand, my fingers brushing his.

His pale eyebrows raised. "Is that so." And he turned to put his back against the bar again.

His hands are so long, Auntie, so sharp. I can feel them as though they were on me now. And all the other places they've been ... the idea of it turned my mouth sour and dry. And now they've settled in one spot. He wasn't looking at his wife, though, as we sat with the hard edge of the bar pressing a slash across our backs. He wasn't looking at his wife and he wasn't looking at me either.

Teffia's song was drawing to a close.

I got up two hours before day
And I got a letter from my true love
And I heard the blackbird and the linnet say
That my love had crossed the ocean

In the splash of applause that followed, Niall took the pint from me once again, drank from it and set it down on the bar-top. He slid off his chair and stepped over to the bodhran player, leaned down to him and said a few words. The bodhran player, his tipper bouncing lightly and quietly on the skin of his drum, cocked his head to one side at me and grinned, a metal tooth in his mouth glinting. He slid over to make a space beside him as Niall took the bodhran out of his hands. The drummer crooked a finger at me and patted the bench.

At the bar and the tables near me men and women broke into applause and hoots. My face was hot as a kettle. The woman sitting next to me put a hand on my shoulder and gave me a gentle shove toward the benches, almost propelling me into Teffia where she stood confused and, from the look of her shutting face, not entirely happy. The bodhran player caught me around the wrist and pulled me down beside him, handing me his little tipper. "Let's see what you can do, girl," he shouted into my ear.

Niall put his hands over mine to press the skin of the drum between them. Shaking his white-gold tail of hair back off his shoulder he smiled and backed toward the bar. I sat motionless for a moment and we gazed at one another, he smiling and me frozen. He waved toward the bodhran and then pressed his palms together and bowed his head, his eyes beseeching over the lips touching the tips of his fingers.

There was a quiet bit of discord as the fiddle and the piano set out. A thin, irregular melody began, something familiar from a long way off. The guitar and the whistle waited for the bodhran to tell them what to do but the bodhran was thinking.

Wasn't this the very music? Michael Mulvaney's arm around his daughter's waist and her arm around his waist, spinning like a cyclone, like a very un-Irish tarantella, their feet thudding sparks and their mouths laughing wide and everyone in the pub laughing and clapping with them.

You could say a lot of things about Michael Mulvaney and I knew that people did, they did say them. One thing was that he could dance. That night he almost crushed me to powder on the stones of the beach I couldn't stop thinking of her body pressed up against his and the two of them whirling like a vortex that swallows everything.

Teffia sank into the chair I'd abandoned by the bar. Niall leaned to say something into her hair but she gave a brusque shake of her head and kept her eyes on me.

I touched the skin of the bodhran gently with the tipper, felt the reverberations too subtle to hear. The whistle joined the fiddle and piano. It was the same tune; I was sure now. I struck the drum experimentally, once and then twice. And then I thought of Teffia closing her eyes and letting the music emerge from her and so that's what I did. I closed my eyes. The tipper in my hand moved against the skin of the bodhran once, twice, three times and then carried itself away.

Rhythm's the thing, Auntie. It's bigger than anything that might get in its way.

I opened my eyes. The fiddler was grinning at me, a flopping handkerchief clutched in his right hand with the bow, and the man at the piano glanced over his shoulder to get a look. His face was thin and young under a mop of dark hair. The bodhran player beside me was drumming on his knees and on the floor with his feet; when I looked his way he opened his eyes and mouth wide in a clownish expression of joy. We thundered away at it and climbed and tightened and sped forever, but the sky outside the window did not break open. There would be no storm tonight.

At the bar Niall was leaning back on his elbows and nodding at the ceiling and Teffia was watching me, her tea-coloured eyes black and wronged. I wished she would dance. I wished I could get up and whippet her around the room myself but I wouldn't know where to start, and in any case I was busy keeping time. The bodhran needs both ends of the tipper, a quick wrist and an elbow that never tires.

Feet were knocking the floor, hands were slapping hands. An old man near the window stood and shuffled across the floor and back again, caught one of the middle-aged tourist women by the hands and pulled her up, spun her around, her face red and teary with laughter. Padraic behind the bar was thumping the bottom of a pint glass against the black bar top, all thoughts of service forgotten. Someone let go a whoop and a cheer rose from the crowd, whistles and pounding and encouraging cries. The piano player turned to look at me again with a guffaw and a bobbing nod of approval. The fiddler's handkerchief flew out of his hand and caught on the end of his bow, flapping like a blue flag in a gale.

A fiddle string snapped.

The room fell every which way with applause. The drummer clapped me on the back and whispered something in Irish in my ear. I think it might have been lewd. I dropped the bodhran back into his lap and planted a kiss on his scruffy cheek. The whistler let his whistle fall to the floor and he pushed me up to take a bow while the fiddler lifted his fiddle and bow into the air and waved them like scorecards.

I moved back toward my chair and Teffia, splashing me with her eyes full of cold dew, stood and stalked from the pub letting the heavy door fall behind her with a quiet thud. No one else seemed to notice her go except for Niall who, after watching the door close, got to his feet, smiled at me, brushed something invisible from his lap and returned to his work.

I slugged back the last of my pint. Niall was moving back and forth, as everyone at the bar seemed to want a drink immediately. The band, as the fiddler fixed his string, was rolling on into a whistling reel and had forgotten me. So I pushed back my chair and made my way toward the door. As I swung it open the tables around me spattered with applause. I turned to give an awkward half-bow and as I looked up I saw Niall at the bar raise his hand in salute. I did the same and moved out into the night.

The air was warmish and busy, the faint odor of fishy salt rising and falling. As I trod the path down to Gilly's house I felt lighter than I have in years, Auntie, and I wanted to tell Gilly. Then I stopped in my tracks and put my hand over my belly.

Don't get any ideas, I told it.

But I'm back at the house now and it's dim and empty, silent except for the sea. I haven't turned on a light; I'm sitting at the kitchen table, sitting and listening. It's almost three in the morning and I should go to bed but I'm not tired; I'm vibrating all over like a refrigerator humming. I left the pub because I didn't want to stay in my chair by the bar, trapped by the smoke and the shouting. I didn't want to stay there and wait for Michael Mulvaney to come and whirl his daughter around the room with her hair flying out. Because what would I do if he did?

It occurs to me now sitting here in Gilly's kitchen that if Michael Mulvaney saw me today he might not even know me.

What I want is to go out for a walk. At first I was afraid to because I don't like the night; you can't see what's in it.

For Christ's sake, what do I have to be afraid of now? The worst anyone can do is kill me.

It made me stop and wonder, that I had to think it out that way.

XI

I shut the door of Gilly's house tight and headed up toward the castle. I was thinking of the total cool black that I remembered inside, the silence, and the winds at the top that try to knock you off. It crumbled above me dark and shattered as I headed up the hill. There were still no stars but the moon was large and bright, making ghosts among the broken stones. Ghosts of people still alive.

I sat on the wall and looked at the ruins for a bit. If I squinted I thought I could see a shadow of a long boney back, of white-blond hair flapping in a churning river, over the broken wall at the very top. *That's it, let down your long hair.* But it was nobody, just the moon touching the remains of everything. I turned around to look out over the sea, to see if there were any ghosts of dead people, but there was nothing but wind and the big moon.

This morning Gilly asked if I'd cried for Mumma, and I said yes. I was telling the truth. I didn't explain that I haven't cried for Mumma since she died, but I often did when she was alive. When she came to take me to live with her again I cried for hours and for days afterwards. She thought it was because I didn't want to leave the Cassatts and go with her; she said that over and over. But it wasn't so simple. Before that, when she came to see me for a day and then went away again, I sometimes cried after she left. Cried until Mrs. Cassatt was afraid I'd make myself sick. It mystifies me even now. Why would I grieve for my mother? It's not like she had anything to give me but the voices of angels and bad promises.

The first thing was that man she called my father.

They don't think I remember that. And I don't remember much. But if I think back to the most distant thing, the thing that entered me and stayed there first of all, it's the sight of the two of them in that bed.

The only person I ever told that to was Teffia. That day out on the rocks on the other side she asked me, "What's the first thing you remember?" Funny how when I think of that day I picture us sitting there in silence until she grabbed my hand and put it up her skirt. But that's not how it happened. She was gazing out to sea and she asked me, "What's the first thing you remember?" and I looked at her, surprised.

I didn't have to think about it; I'd worked it out many times and I knew exactly what I'd say if anyone asked me that question. I had to consider whether I'd say it, though, because it was no more her business than anyone else's. But she seemed like the right person. I said, "My mother having sex with a man in a bed in a dark room."

Teffia's eyebrows arched and her lips curled in a half-sneer smile. Still watching the waves she asked, "Did she know you were there?"

I shrugged. "Probably," I said.

Teffia looked at me then and a pulse went through me; I wanted to lean over and kiss those wide lips. I had never before wanted to kiss anyone so thoughtlessly and so hard. I couldn't, though. I couldn't imagine anything more wrong than that.

"Is it angry with her you are then?"

What is she asking? I wondered. I didn't answer her. We looked at each other for a while. Every bit of me was racing; I thought I was shaking but then I lifted a hand a centimetre from where it was resting on my thigh and it was steady.

"I know," she said. She gave a wisp of a sigh. "People believe you should be angry. But if you think of it, there's no reason. Animals do it in front of each other all the time."

She grasped my steady hand then, but when she leaned over and tried to put her lips on mine I couldn't let her. The rest of it was all right by me but not that.

I do remember him; I remember being afraid. He was a big man and although his voice was quiet it was hard and strained as though it might burst. He never spoke to me and when he looked at me I felt like glass. Until the police came I thought I was a figment of my mother's imagination. He was a good man, Mumma used to tell me. He took care of us and he was a good father. A good father to who? I wondered. I didn't ask. But I'm asking you now, Auntie. A good father to who?

Someone was floating up the path toward me.

Who the hell would come out here at four in the morning? I wondered. Kids maybe, sneaking out of their houses to drink whiskey and have sex. Or maybe not. This person was a white wraith and her hair glowed copper like a lunar eclipse.

She was smiling and she came up close to where I was sitting. Her feet were still bare and must have been cold against the damp dark rocks and gravel. I swung around to follow her with my eyes as she moved through the broken dip near me in the wall.

"Here." Teffia stood between me and the door of the castle and motioned, the same motion as the other day on the beach, her arm raising and pulling the air toward her. With the moon beside her I could see the shape of her straight through her dress. "Let me show you."

I didn't move. "Show me what?"

"Come see, then." Her face was in shadow but I imagined her mouth wry and mocking.

My belly pulsed. *I think I already know.*

Teffia disappeared inside.

I sat for a moment longer staring after her. The air was cooling rapidly. As clouds moved over the moon the black outline of the castle seemed to shiver and shift and draw in on itself. Maybe the whole thing would collapse on us if I went in, like the universe sucked into the vortex of a dancing man and his daughter's red hair.

I stood and followed Teffia inside.

The middle room of the castle was almost opaque black, but light must have come from somewhere to glow faintly on her white dress. Her back against the wall. "Over here."

I didn't move. "I was just sitting. I didn't ask for company. I thought you were with Gillian."

"Come now, no one will know."

"No." The word scraped at the walls.

Teffia's voice oboe-like, amused. "Ah, you will."

She pulled away from the wall and like a moonbeam flowed up to me. Her body was not like a moonbeam; it was warm and thick with breath. She wrapped a hand around the back of my neck. Here inside the dark we might have been the only two people left alive. Teffia took my hand and slid it up under the white dress between soft legs.

"Come now," Teffia murmured. "It never takes me more than a minute, but I'll do you for as long as you want."

I tried to think as I ran my hand over the slickness of her and listened, wished I could see her face the way it was that day on the rocks so long ago ... I pulled my hand away.

She slid her hands up under my shirt and I concentrated on the slim bones over my swollen breasts. Will she notice, I wondered, the suspicion of my belly? Then she pushed me down into the cold dirt and pulled my skirt up a bit roughly and my underpants down, tossed them away somewhere into the dark.

"Why are you so unkind?" My voice was too hard, echoing a little and then sucked away by the pores of the stones.

She froze. Her moist breath was poised above the fur between my legs. Slowly she pushed my knees apart. Her lips brushed a hair or two and shocks travelled from the core of me out toward my skin.

"Unkind, is it?" she barely whispered. "We'll see."

Then her tongue descended; her hands clutched me open where my legs meet the rest of me.

I knew what she was aiming for. She wanted me to do what she'd done that day, to writhe and scream and moan and then lie still. I'd seen it in movies and read of it in books; I'd even known enough to try to make it happen by myself. But I didn't believe that I had it in me.

She was, however, true to her word, and that surprised me. It seemed to take forever but after a minute or two I did-n't mind that. She went at me with slow deliberation, long wet strokes that never seemed to grow tired. I closed my eyes and tried to forget that it was her, imagined that it was Niall, that it was Gilly. But soon I knew that I wanted it to be her, that if anyone ever tried to do this to me again I would imag-ine her in their place. It started to ache out in all directions, pulled me to the dirt ground and the ceiling stones and the ocean and her mouth all at once and when I let go with a cracked "O" she slid a hard finger inside me and then two and sucked with a pull and plunge until the baby itself pleaded for her to finish me off and my whole life broke into fragments the size of her teeth, set free a yell that shot out all the broken doors of the castle and fell over the whole island, jarred it a few inches deeper into the sea.

She knew to keep her tongue at it a moment more, slowed and curled, withdrew her hand and let me pulse and burn and finally pull away. Then she drew herself up and settled her bare mound over mine, her legs folded tight on either side of me, the soft peach inner lips of her nudging against me warm and firm and she circled a little with her hips, and her breath started to roll in mountains right from her depths and it was no time at all before her hands pinned my hair to the earth and she moaned into my mouth and I rose up once again to meet her and the two of us shook and cried out into one another, until finally she crumbled onto me and we lay in a heap of sweat-damp rags and soil and worn-out white skin.

If I had the slightest doubt that I don't deserve to live I'm free of it now.

She rolled off me and we lay quietly for a while side by side, our arms barely touching, her hair tangled in mine between our faces. I thought of the afternoons when she and Gilly would fight in a language I didn't understand, quiet and vicious as knives; sometimes she made Gilly cry but when I asked Gilly what it was about she told me to shut up. I thought of Niall saying, "There wouldn't be a man on this island who hasn't been with Teffia Mulvaney."

She laughed.

"What?" I asked; it broke as it moved through my throat.

"You," she said.

"What about me?"

"You being so sure that you wouldn't."

I didn't want her to go. I didn't want her to run off the way she had that other time. I turned on my side and propped myself up on my elbow, trying to make out her white outline against the black earth. But I could see nothing. I reached out and felt the rough thin cotton of her dress, tried to slip a finger between two buttons to the skin inside, but she picked my hand up lightly and put it away from her.

"Why do you do such things?" I asked.

"Because I like it," she said. "Don't you?"

The earth beneath us was growing colder by the second, dampening the back of my clothes. I imagined myself returning home to find Gilly waiting, imagined myself trying to explain the stains of soil.

"You like it with everyone?" I asked.

"I do."

The laughter left her voice then. She lay very still. I listened to the sea trying to shout through the broken walls.

"I have never understood," she said slowly, "why people can't take things for what they are."

Silence.

I sat up, peeling my damp shirt away from my back, but then my strength left me and I sank down again a little closer to her than before. She didn't move away.

"Like Gilly, you mean?"

I felt her head shake slowly; her hair moved against the side of my face. "No," she said. Her voice sweet and soft and deep was like singing even when she spoke. "Not Gilly. People." She shifted. "You for one. And that boy Niall too. Do you know what he said to me tonight?" I waited. "He said,

'Stay away from that one, Teffie.'" I felt her arm move, saw a vague shimmer of a white hand rise and stretch above our heads.

Niall at the bar leaning into Teffia's hair and her head with its short brutal shake, coppery waves pushing his face away.

Out of the darkness rose the moment of passing them on the beach, a black greasy head and a cloud of sunrise waves glowing in the heat which moved in the air like oil. The blank expanse of grey and white rocks, the chutes of black weeds, the sky thin sapphire.

"I want to know something," I said.

I told her about the spot not far from the *Plassy* and the man and the girl I saw amongst the rocks, the moustached man and the red-haired girl. So long ago now and I don't trust any of my memories of that time any more, I can't be certain that I didn't make everything up, the whole summer just one more thing that I wished for so hard that I came to believe it. But of anything I saw or heard, that man and that girl on the rocks out by the *Plassy* are the most real, the sun on her hair and his feet on either side of her head. I may have imagined everything else but I didn't imagine that.

"Was it you?" I asked.

She didn't answer me for a moment.

Then she said softly, "You see? This is what I'm saying. If I want to do something, and it doesn't hurt anyone, why do people think they have something to say about it?"

"If you want to do what?"

She pulled away a little, turned on her side. In the almost-black light I saw an outline of her valentine face turned toward me.

"I came with himself like I did with anyone else," she said.

The sea laughed like birds.

I was starting to shiver with cold, wanted to pull down my skirt, to get up and find my underpants, to go home and tell Gilly I was sorry. But I didn't dare move.

She said, "Animals do it to each other all the time, like. How do you think they made us in the first place? Of course when they look at us they can't help thinking of us as little packets of sex. I can't really blame them."

She was watching me. I could feel it although I didn't know how she could see me in the dark or what she was looking for.

Mumma fell with arms outstretched from the paste of night toward me, screaming like a seagull against the starless moonless sky.

So low I imagined she might not even hear, I said, "Why was it my mother?"

I felt her shrug. "Your mother what?"

I didn't answer.

"Who died, is that it?"

The stones breaking my back to ribbons and then his back firm and satisfied wandering away from me along the beach as though he had just finished lunch and was off to work again.

"Because Gilly knew," Teffia said, "that I could stop loving her just as easy as I started. But you ... you don't seem to be the kind who stops loving anyone."

The moondim edges of her faces descended with a cold bruising kiss. "But it doesn't matter now, does it?" she whispered against my hair. With a white rustle all her warmth pulled away and out.

I lay alone on the cold earth of the castle floor and for a while I cried, listening to the ocean. It was a little like being here that first time with Niall but he'd stayed with me then and helped me not to cry. He hadn't left me alone with the wind waiting upstairs to eat me alive.

When I finally calmed my heart and got to my feet I couldn't find my underpants in the darkness. I pulled my skirt straight, tried to brush the dirt from my clothes, ran my fingers through the knots in the back of my hair. Then I made my way out of the castle, bumping myself a few times on the rough stones of the walls, and down the hill to Gilly's house, shivering in the clammy breeze.

A light shone through the kitchen window. When I came through the door Gilly was at the table, the red King James open before her. I tried to say something, to say good evening or to ask her where she'd been. But she didn't look up. Her elbows were on the table and her face rested motionless between her hard fists. I stood and watched her for a moment but she didn't speak, didn't even turn a page. Finally I turned into the little alcove where my bed was waiting, stripped off my earthstained clothes, folded myself under the covers and tried to fall asleep, listening to her silent reading of the Good Book.

FIVE

Rosary

XII

I never loved Molly as I should have. She was frightening really. From the time she was born, my father insisted she was an angel of some kind. O, of course I was jealous; how could I help it? My mother and I were just women to him, meant for woman sorts of things, teaching and taking care of babies. Molly was meant for God. Not that I envy her that in the end. That was what turned her into such a nutter.

No, there's no other way about it, Clare, and I'm sorry, it's not a nice thing to say about someone's mother, certainly. But she was my sister too, you know. O yes, pretty doesn't come close to describing it. Even as a newborn she was an exquisite little doll-like thing, and then she got that pile of yellow curls, and all those brown limbs. When her breasts came in you'd see grown men stop dead in the street; shameful it was, looking that way at a little girl. I've no doubt that if she had a big nose, or if she'd been fat, my father never would have thought to call her the Lamb of God.

You look quite a lot like her, Clare. Plumper, certainly, and paler and without that otherworldly sort of look that made men want to pin her down on the earth. But your eyes, and the shape of your mouth. It's strange, that you can look so much like her and so much like your father too: your hair's the same wavy dark and your nose ...

O yes, I know all about that Immaculate Conception business. When Mother Agnes called and told me about Molly claiming she was carrying the child of God, I thought about going home. Our baby had died by then after all, and it seemed clear Colin didn't have much use for me any longer. But then we learned Gilly was coming. It had been a long wait, and suddenly Colin and I had a reason to be together again. So we wrote and told the nuns that we'd bring you both over once Gilly was there and everything was settled and in order. And Colin got sick just after Gilly arrived and there was all that. And by the time it was possible for me to go, you and your mother were nowhere to be found.

I thought maybe I should go home just to be there, to be a sort of beacon waiting for her. But after Colin died I realized I couldn't leave Inisheer. It had become my home, and Gilly's home too. I mentioned to her once that maybe we could go live in Newfoundland, and that evening — all of three years old she was — she left the house all alone and walked out to the *Plassy*, climbed up inside and fell to the rocks below. The tide was out and she had nothing but a few bruises, but I knew what it was all about. One of the villagers saw her heading in that direction, and when I went off in a panic, going from house to house looking for her, he walked me along the beach and we saw her lying on the stones. The seconds when I thought she might be dead were the longest I've ever known. I knew what it was about.

Ah yes, I'm sorry, I got lost a little there. No, no darling. It was Father Corrigan, there's no doubt in my mind. She mentioned him in her letters more often than I liked: going to see him about this and that, how kind he was, and so on. He was arrested a few years later on charges from a whole mess of girls, but Molly was long gone by then. One of the only priests I ever knew who preferred little girls to little boys. I'm sorry darling, that's a cruel joke. It's not a laughing matter, I'm well aware. It was a shock to everybody; he was a young and handsome man, very kind to everyone, I'd fancied him myself before I met Colin, but Father Corrigan never looked twice at me in that way, although he was always very friendly. I put it down to his being a priest, and honourable.

Do you remember anything at all about St. Margaret's? It was a strange place, looking back, with all those rich girls mixed in with all those orphans. And Molly and I were first rich and then orphans, although by the time Mum and Dad died I was too old to be an orphan really, old enough to look after myself, although it must have been hard for Molly. She always said it was all right, they were with God and that was best, and I never had the heart to say that if God stuck to His rules they weren't with Him at all, or at least Dad wasn't. O, Dad talked often about how he was not meant for this world; too miserable for this world more likely — I said that to him once and got a wallop to the side of my head for my trouble. No, Clare, your grandfather was not a nice man. Molly was too young to understand, never seemed to have noticed that he beat our mother senseless. He never laid a hand on Molly. I don't think it was a coincidence that he made sure she was well cared for and went directly to drive himself and Mum off the side of a cliff. O, I can look back now and say it easily, but at the time I thought I might go mad myself, crying every night over my poor Mum.

O, we weren't close, don't misunderstand. I left home for school when Molly'd barely been born. I only saw her in the summertimes and at Christmas, and once I turned fourteen, and could work at St. Margaret's in the summers, Dad was all too happy to leave me there when I asked. But when she started school I felt an obligation to her.

Well, now. Let me be honest. I was frightened of her even then; she seemed possessed, as though she was full of demons that had convinced her they were angels. We learned later it was all medical, or mostly. But in a way I was rather proud under everything. She was so beautiful, you see, it would stop your heart, it really would, and what's more, although she had the meanest temper you ever saw — she bit a nun once who was trying to cut off her hair — when she was sweet it was a real sweetness, not put on the way some girls do it to get what they want. She wasn't at all the sort to be devious or to manipulate. Either people gave her anything she asked for or she went out of her head and screamed and kicked.

I can only imagine what happened with that pervert who kept her locked up for almost five years — O Clare, O God, maybe this isn't something you want discussed. Do you remember all that? Of course, you were still a baby then. I don't know what was in her mind, but when they finally found her, the story goes, she didn't want to go with them. She loved him, she said. I try to imagine the two of you shut away like that, her using old T-shirts because he didn't dare buy diapers at the store. But I can imagine what happened. She chanced upon him somewhere, and he took one look at her, and all his brains dropped straight into his prick. Shame on him, a little girl like that. And she didn't have to do a thing, just presented herself to be rescued. From what, I'm sure I don't know.

I do believe it was that family who saved you, the ones they sent you to while she was in the hospital. What were their names? I talked to them occasionally, and they seemed like such lovely people. Weren't they lovely people? It's the only explanation I can find for why you're not dead or in jail or a complete fruitcake like your mother. Isn't it strange, Clare, how you turned out so strong, and Gilly ... well, that's another story, isn't it. But I can tell you one thing, Clare. Your grandmother would be proud of you if she were alive.

Yes, Gilly told me everything. Why do you suppose we left for England after you were gone? I don't know if you've ever lived in a place like Inisheer, but it's not the sort of spot you want to be if people think you're a scandal. And Gilly went ahead and went back home anyway, all over that Mulvaney girl. O, I don't judge; after the things we've seen, my daughter being a lesbian is the least of my troubles, I can tell you. I still love her with all my heart after everything; she's a good girl deep down, Gilly is, no matter what shows on the surface. I have to tell you, Clare, I've never caused harm to anyone in my life, never kicked a dog and never struck my children more than a little tap on the bum, but if I'd seen what Gilly saw I might have killed your mother myself, Clare. I wouldn't have calculated it as Gilly did, mind you, but I might very well have picked up a stone off the beach and crushed her pretty head. Forgive me, darling. But when Gilly finished telling, for a moment I felt nothing but relief that Molly was dead.

But as for Michael Mulvaney ... do you see what my problem was? How was I to say anything? It would have been very easy for the connections to be made, and Gilly was too volatile, she wasn't shrewd, she was sure to say something to implicate herself. It was cowardly of me, Clare, I know that now. Gilly was still a child; her punishment wouldn't likely have been more than what one deserves for killing a woman. But I couldn't see my daughter taken away from me, Clare. Seeing as who your mother was, that might be hard for you to hear. But Molly felt the same way for you, no matter what kind of love it might have been.

In the meantime Gilly's back there, and the laughingstock of Inisheer, although it's nothing to do with Molly now, I suppose. I wish to God she'd go back to London, where it's easier just to be one more face with a nasty invisible history. But I think that as long as Teffia is alive Gilly will be with her. They've known each other since they were tiny children, and I remember walking on them playing their little sex games when they were hardly old enough to know what any of it meant, and more than once. It did worry me, I admit, but I put it down to normal childish curiosity. I wasn't very comfortable discussing that sort of thing. I'm still not, although I've recovered from many of my discomforts over the years. I've never seen anyone love anyone the way Gilly loves Teffia, and no good will come of it, I'm convinced of that. O, she cares for Gilly as much as she knows how to care for anyone, I imagine. But since she was old enough to walk, she's laid down on every patch of soil to be found on the island, and most of the hard rocks too, with just about every boy or man who didn't have the fibre to say no, and more girls than just Gilly I gather, and she's broken the hearts of more than one. She's got no love in her, that girl. It's amazing what this thing called beauty can do for a woman. Those of us who don't have it will never know that kind of power. Teffia and your mother were of a kind that way, although at least Molly did not have malice. Teffia's a mean one, Clare, and I can't say I blame her when I look at her life, but I wish to God she'd get the hell away from my daughter.

O, I've tried, Clare, I've tried. I've tried at least to get her to stop shooting up that cheap smack she buys off the boats;

I wake up nights cold and sweating, having dreamt she died on the beach in a pool of her own vomit. And in the end it was that, I suppose, that broke me down.

What I really want is to be back home. Home on Inisheer, I mean; that's my home now, and the past is past enough that I think I would be all right there. I've thought of going back to Newfoundland, too, more than once, but Molly's shadow would be everywhere. The bad memories won't go away, and there are days when I think of my Dad, and think maybe he did the most sensible thing. But I don't think the world needs saving from me, Clare. After everything, I think I've come through all right. You and I are of a kind that way.

SIX

Clare

XIII

Niall came here yesterday in the evening. Gilly was inside with her Bible. I was lying across the doorstep in my yellow dress from Galway, my feet bare and my head in the spare uncut weed-grass, my face up to the pale nine o'clock light. Every evening I expect it to get dark at a reasonable hour and every evening the sun stays up and up and hovers and teases. I like it. I've never liked the dark. I was trying to decide whether I wanted to spend one more night at the pub or what, and there he was standing over me, his face and hair all shadows against the stone-milk sky.

As I looked up at him one of the small planes started up on the landing pad below near the beach; I could hear it whirr, grind, then purr along. As I watched it pass over his head I remembered sitting five years ago in the window of the plane from Shannon to St. John's, looking down as it took off and wondering if he still stood in the airport where I'd left him, if he was looking out as my plane flew away. Sitting by the window, looking down at my hands where the copper ring he'd bought me in a Galway souvenir shop the day before was already turning my finger green. Thinking: *Why didn't he say I could stay with him? Why did he let me go?*

I said, "Not working tonight?"

"Nor you, it seems." He grinned, a faint movement in the shadow of his face. "Grainne's at the bar for me this evening."

I sat up and pulled the stretching yellow dress up around my thighs so I could sit cross-legged, telling myself in the middle of the movement not to care about the soft white flesh

I was exposing. "You put her to work so you could come to see me? Or maybe you're here by accident."

"No, I've come to see you."

"And why is that?" I rested my elbows on my knees, thought of the yoga class I used to take and tried to breathe serenity into my diaphragm.

"To see how you're doing is all." He patted the worn khaki backpack hanging on his shoulder. "I've a nice firm toke and a bottle of whiskey, if you'd like to share with me. Just a puff and a glass for you, though, in your condition."

"Sounds nice." My stomach was a blizzard. I stretched my legs out, smoothed my dress down over my knees, then noted that all of my shuffling betrayed nerves and frowned myself still. "You shouldn't let her work on her feet in that pub full of smoke."

He laughed a bit roughly. "You're not one to be giving me lectures on the proper treatment of pregnancies. Come on, now."

"Where are we going?"

"Where do you think? To commune with the spirits."

It was a cool still evening and voices floated from the beach and from the village as we picked our way down to the graveyard to sit on the wall of the temple of Saint Kevin. Below by the water a few tourists stretched themselves on the cold sand, probably discussing a late dinner or a pint. Niall slung one leg over the wall of the temple and so did I, hitching my yellow dress up around my thighs again. We sat with a little decent space between our knees.

What is it about men, Auntie? I could look at him from every angle and he was not at all beautiful, his face all craggy and his teeth broken, but it didn't matter a bit. It wasn't like it was with Teffia where all I cared about were the shapes and colours of her. And Gilly's something else altogether. But sitting there, our legs on either side of the wall as he lit the toke carefully and his moonlight hair fell around him in the white dusk, I thought: *I could wait my whole life for this.*

A couple of people loitered above us in the graveyard looking at tombstones: a youngish couple, the woman plump in a long dark dress, the man skinny and bespectacled and silent, snapping a fancy automatic camera while the woman kept her back to him, chattering about something I couldn't quite distinguish until she turned around and cried, "Would you stop wasting the film on all those shitty pictures!"

"Aren't you concerned someone could see you taking off with the tourist girls while your pregnant wife slogs behind the bar?" I asked.

He puffed and handed the toke to me. "We're smoking and talking is all, Clare," he said, "and Grainne usually works on Tuesdays. She'll finish up early and leave the closing to Padraic. I'm not here to seduce you, darling, I just wanted to talk a bit."

"All right." Something in my throat sank. "All right, then."

He smiled. It was a kind smile, sympathetic but not altogether respectful, the way you might smile at a child who's just learned there's no Santa Claus.

"I am well and truly married now, Clare. Sorry about that. If I'd known you were waiting for me, I might have thought twice."

My cheeks went hot as boiling milk. "Fuck you, Niall."

He shrugged and drew his mouth into a gentle line. "I'm just taking the piss out of you. But we're out here where we can be seen because I don't want to foment any gossip. I thought we had a bit of catching up to do is all."

"I don't see why."

A movement of the evening air cooled me abruptly. I hadn't brought my jacket; my dress was too thin and sunny for such a night. It made me think of Teffia careening around in her little slips of white cotton but I'm sure on me it didn't work so well. Niall must have seen me shiver, because he took off his sweater and handed it to me. (His jumper you'd call it, now that you've been here so long. I almost wrote that but I'm not quite Irish yet. Sweater is an ugly word though, I realize.) I considered resisting but I put it on.

Above us on the road a gang of kids, boys and girls between fifteen and twenty, swarmed along laughing and bitching. They were speaking English but a voice sounded Irish and then another was indecipherably foreign. One of the bigger boys snatched a girl up around the waist and ran up the hill with her tucked under his arm, her limbs splayed, bobbing like a blow-up doll; she shrieked and kicked and jabbed with her elbows. They shrank slowly along the lines of the land but I could still hear them shouting.

Niall sighed and unscrewed the cap of the whiskey bottle. "I know about your little plan."

The joint fell from my fingers. My eyes followed it as it bounced off the crumbled wall and fell onto the moist packed dirt deep in the temple. Without a word Niall propped the whiskey bottle against a stone, swung his legs over and dropped off the wall into the ground. He emerged with the joint, which was now a little moist and dirty, and swung himself over the wall again.

"Grass may be cheap where you come from, love," he said,

"but it's after travelling a long way to come here." He brushed the dirt off the paper with the tips of his fingers and tried to light the joint again without much success.

"What plan?"

It lit finally and he puffed at it, smoke billowing from his lips. I held out my hand but he drew back and shook his head. "I'll not have you throwing my hard-earned drugs into the earth. Your plan to tip yourself off the *Plassy.*"

Damn Gillian. "That's ridiculous."

"Is it, then?"

I snatched the bottle of whiskey before he could stop me. "Who told you such a thing?"

I took a long swig and wiped my mouth with the sleeve of his sweater, which made him smile but his face went serious again. "Teffia did."

"Teffia?" That stopped me short, the bottle dangling in my hand. "How would Teffia know?"

He laughed. "For Christ's sake, Clare." He sucked on the joint and exhaled in a warm grey stream. "Have you ever been in love with someone?"

"No." The baby kicked me. *Goddammit,* I thought. *Not now.*

Niall's eyebrows, which are almost as pale as his hair, arched. "Well, it makes secrets hard to keep."

"Gillian had no right."

"Maybe not." He held his hand out for the whiskey bottle, which I passed him, and he extended the joint. When I reached toward it he pulled away and looked at me meaningfully.

"I won't drop it," I said.

He gave it to me. "So you're thinking it's all over now," he said, and took a drink.

"Yes."

"I see."

"We made a promise."

"Aye, Teffie told me that story too. But you were children, Clare, and things were very bad at that time." He looked out toward the ocean and raised his chin at it as if wondering what it was making of this conversation.

In the distance I could still hear the cries and laughter of the gang of teenagers. I wondered if that girl was still propped under that boy's arm, both of them happy to touch someone and be touched.

I said, "Things will always be very bad, my love."

I don't know how that slipped out. He smiled, still staring at the ocean over his shoulder. Embarrassed, I continued. "Don't tell anyone."

"What should I not tell anyone?" He leaned back on one hand, the other hand dangling the whiskey bottle, his wide eyes holding me in place. The breeze was moving his hair around him. "You don't expect me to let you go and die."

"You've got nothing to say about it. But I meant about Gilly."

He looked away again, gave another little sigh, pushed his mane of shifting hair off his face with one hand.

"Everybody knows, Clare, that your mother did not jump off the *Plassy* of her own accord."

A bang and a shout came down the hill behind us, and we both turned. Far above us on the hotel steps, so far that we could barely distinguish one from the other in the coming dark, two men had crashed out through the pub door and were hanging on to one another and howling with laughter, each with a pint in one hand. They gasped and crowed in

Irish and then it seemed one of them saw us and raised his glass in our direction. "It's the golden-haired Niall!" he roared, and then continued to shout in Irish as Niall raised a hand and smiled a wan smile. Finally a pair of hands emerged from the doorway, grabbed each of the patrons by the collar and hauled them back inside. "You're quite the man, Niall my son!" bellowed the disappearing man as the door slammed shut.

I handed the joint back to him and he puffed at it a bit. I waited for him to give me the whiskey but he didn't. I waited for him to say something but he didn't. So finally I asked, "What do you mean, everybody knows?"

He turned and furrowed his brow at me as though he thought I was just asking questions to be difficult.

"Why do you suppose Gillian Flaherty never leaves her green house?" He flicked ashes from the joint with vehemence. "Why do you suppose her one friend is the Happy Hooker of Inisheer? The only surprise is that she's still here, and that redhead harpy is the reason." He settled back on his hands, satisfied, the butt of the joint poking from between his fingers.

I snorted. "Ah, love."

"Call it what you like."

What else is there to call it? I thought. Want, I suppose. It's just words in any case. No one — not even Gilly, I'd be willing to bet — would ever have thought that she and Teffia would still want each other five years later. It's the sort of thing you read about, the sort of thing everybody always fantasizes will happen to them but convinces themselves never will because they want protection from the disappointment they think is inevitable.

Or maybe it's the opposite. Maybe most people have to believe that things last and then are proven wrong.

Niall was growing ruffled and salty in the sea wind, his blue eyes wide and deep under silvery hair. The toke was burning low and I wanted some more before it was gone, but when I stretched my hand toward him he ignored me. "Everyone knows everything here, Clare. If the *gardai* don't know — and they might — it's because they don't stay here. It's more likely they do know but they don't feel there's any need to do anything about it."

He took one last puff and flicked the end of the joint. It plummeted into the depths at the center of the temple, then lay still and burned like a resting firefly.

"What else do people know?" I asked.

"Such as?"

"Well, do you know why?"

"Why what?"

"Why Mumma died."

"About you and Teffia's father? I do. Teffie told me about that a long time ago. But I don't think there's too many who know that story." He swallowed some whiskey.

"And you don't think the *gardai* need to bother themselves with that either, I suppose."

"With Michael Mulvaney?" Niall peered into the neck of the bottle as if surprised by the taste of the stuff and wondering if it was not what he'd thought it was. "Michael Mulvaney should have been sterilized and hog-tied at birth. But there's not much to be done now."

"What the hell is that supposed to mean?"

He looked at me, the bottle still near his face. "Mulvaney's dead, Clare. Died not a month after you left and Gilly and her mother took off for England. Hanged himself."

And he passed the bottle to me.

I swung both my legs to the side of the temple wall that faced the sea. Beside us the spattering of graves with stones of all sizes and shades of grey rose like a cresting wave, the couple still meandering, the man silent and the woman gabbing; a phrase or two floated down: " ... back to Doolin tomorrow where there's something to fucking do ... "

The world was losing its dimensions. The stars and the waves and Galway pulled toward us; the graves above were no closer than the horizon. I rubbed my eyes and could barely feel my fingers. I looked down into the temple and thought I could reach out and press the flat of my hand onto the earth below my feet, but when I tried I touched only empty air. I shivered again but I hardly knew why; I didn't feel cold. I didn't feel anything. In any case Niall had no more sweaters to give me.

"Why did he do that?" I asked, looking up at him. His head was solid against the flat cartoon backdrop of the sky.

He laughed, a short bark. "Makes you think his God was a just one in the end." It was growing dim now; it must have been close to eleven o'clock. Niall's face was craggy with new shadows. "Or that Mulvaney started to believe in earthly consequences." He raised his eyes to mine. "Killing oneself is not a brave thing, Clare."

I looked away from him and down into the temple again. *The ground down there is much farther away than it seems. I'd probably hurt myself if I fell.* Not if I jumped but if I fell, by accident.

"What about killing someone else?" I asked.

"About that I don't know."

The sunken temple was filling with darkness like a pool filling with water. What once were walls had become nothing but borders, memories made of rock.

"You don't get it, Niall."

"Get what?" He was staring down into the temple too, swinging his heels in their battered boots against the wall.

"What it is to be full of poison. Everything I touch dies or goes rotten."

"You touched me, love, and I'm still here."

All the blood in me pounded and stopped. He looked up at me almost coyly, his long pale waves of hair falling away from his face and whipping themselves into knots in the sea wind.

I wanted to run a finger across his thin lips and see what he would do. *Surely he hasn't changed as much as he pretends.* I was about to lift my hand from the wall but he shifted and his hair fell across his face and I was suddenly afraid of what would happen to me if I made him say no.

"Why are you still here, Niall?"

His blue eyes were going grey as the light faded. "What do you mean?"

"Here on Inisheer. And don't tell me about that four-eyed mouse of yours."

He frowned. "What a miserable thing to say. You don't know her. She's a good woman."

"She's not the kind of girl who ever meant a thing to you."

Niall raised his eyebrows, and pulled a pack of Sweet Aftons from the pocket of his T-shirt. Even in the cold breeze there wasn't so much as a goosebump under the gold down of his forearms. I stretched out a hand. He held the cigarettes away from me and shook his head, but I fixed him with a steady look and kept my hand extended. Finally he relented, offered the pack, pulled out his lighter and lit both our cigarettes in one motion. I spat a few shreds of tobacco and coughed.

"Those little blond things from Paris and Stockholm, is that what you're talking about? But you weren't like them either, Clare, and of all of them I liked yourself best." I blushed and opened my mouth. "No, that is the truth, I'm not just saying it because you're the one I'm talking to. You weren't as handsome or as glamorous as the Sophies and the Gretels and the Lucias, but you were something to me."

I looked down at the blue of his sweater stretched tight across my big breasts, at the ripple of the butter-yellow hem against my heavy legs. The prickly soft knobs of my ankles sticking out of my dirty tennis shoes. *He can't be serious.*

He paused for a long moment, his face fighting with itself, his lips opening slightly and then closing.

"That day I took you to Shannon," he said finally.

Rising into the sky and leaving my insides behind where I hoped he was standing at the airport window and watching me go. But very probably he'd turned around and headed back to the bus which would take him to Galway and to the boat which would take him back to his life. I didn't want to know which was true. Again I almost raised a hand and pressed it across his mouth, this time to stop him from saying any more. But I couldn't move.

"That day I put you on the plane, I thought of asking you to stay. It wouldn't have been easy, jamming you in with me and Da and the two sisters, but I didn't fancy letting you go right away.

"But I didn't know if I would ... love you. I hardly knew

you. And I knew that something was gone to crap. You looked so bruised and emptied out. I was afraid."

I bit my lips together and stared down into the earth at the bottom of the temple, rising toward me; I thought I could still see a faint glow of a burning spot of weed swimming upwards in the darkness. I ground the tips of my fingers against the ancient crumble of stone which held me just inches above the land behind me.

"Do you remember that ring I bought for you?"

I nodded but I didn't look at him. I tried to speak, to tell him that I'd worn it for all those years, but I didn't seem to have any breath in me. I could hear the young couple leaving the graveyard and wandering down the road, not talking, not liking one another much.

"I didn't want that you'd forget me," he said.

I tossed my Sweet Afton into the temple and put the whiskey bottle to my mouth.

"When I met Grainne ... well, not when I met her. I have to say, Clare, after a year or so I didn't think of you much any more. Gilly and Rosary had gone away to England, so there weren't many reminders. But since you've come back, I've been remembering, and I notice things about herself that are like you. On the outside she's very sure of things, sure that she knows what she wants. But there's a wavering under-neath. It took a long time for me to believe that she wanted us to marry, because although she said it with great convic-tion I could see that she hadn't thought it through.

"But then one night we sat out on the pier with some friends. It was just when her Irish was coming to full flower; she could talk to people and they forgot she wasn't one of us. She was laughing and drinking and her face was all lit up with the moon and everyone was teasing her that she didn't want to be stuck with an eejit like me. And she looked at me and she said, 'But I do, lads.'"

He pronounced something softly in Irish.

"'But I do, lads.' And I knew that this was the first time she'd said it truly."

He took the whiskey bottle from my hand.

Bile was rising in my throat. *So that's all it takes.* Forgetting. It seems easy for most people: when something goes away they forget. And then something else comes along.

"You're here because this is where she wants to be," I said.

He swallowed, spluttered, wiped his mouth and shook his head. "Quite the opposite."

"Niall." I gave a short laugh. "You can't really want to spend your whole life on this tiny rock in the middle of nowhere. You could have gone to university. You're made for more than this."

His eyes were on the sea, the shake of his head tense and minimal. "That's where you're dead wrong. I'm not made *for* anything; the most I am is made *of* something."

He offered me the pack of cigarettes with a blind automatic gesture, not looking my way. I took one. So did he, and lit them both again, never taking his eyes off the cold close churning of the horizon. Then he sighed and leaned back on his hands again.

"I tried Galway, Clare. I tried England. I even went to Boston for a few months. Americans bore me, with their Coca-Cola petty values and their hundred-and-five channels. The English bore me with their tight-ass chin-up pasty faces. Even the Irish bore me with their talk of *Sinn Fein,* children learning to speak the Irish without a clue what it really means. You know what I saw?"

His eyes were grey as the water in the fading light.

"When I was working in Galway I went to a football match between Galway and Manchester schools. They were huddled and one of the little Galway lads backed out and bawled at the English team ... " and here Niall bellowed something in Irish. His voice bounced off the walls and the gravestones and ricocheted down across the sand and the water, as if there were still some depth to the world. I thought I heard a sudden silence and then a guffaw from the teenagers still gallivanting in the distance. "Do you know what that means?" he returned to me. "It means, 'Sausages are tasty and I like ice cream.' I got on the boat home that very night, left my contract without a word to anyone.

"This is my home, Clare. I'll be pushing coffee and Smithwick's in that hotel pub until the day I die or until I'm too old to stand, and then my children or my neighbours or God will look after me. You may not think much of my life, but you haven't the slightest notion. This may be the only real world left as far as I can see."

He pushed his hair off his face with one hand. With the other he put the cigarette to his lips. I watched him and wondered if I was remembering correctly what the touch of those lips was like, how that hair felt under my hands.

He turned his eyes on me again. "All you want is a place," he said. "There's no poison in you, love. You need a place, and so does that baby of yours."

He tossed his cigarette into the ruins and stood up, a cutout gainst the darkening sky, weedy and bent; the wind pulled at his clothes. I took off his sweater and handed it to him. A blue sweater knitted in Aran patterns; I wondered for a moment if Grainne had made it for him.

"Right now," he said — and once again his crooked smile flicked through the shadows of his face — "I wish I'd met you one more time before I chose to get a wife. But there's nothing to be done about that. Understand, though, Clare: if you decide that living is a better option, there are worse places you could do it than Inisheer."

He turned and walked away up the hill toward Gilly's house, toward the hotel where his wife was working at the bar, toward the other side of the island which faces the place I come from.

I sat and watched him and waited for the world to reclaim all its dimensions. But everything kept on staring at me like a hanging portrait stares at you; I felt that if I stood and walked around the stone wall in front of me I would walk around the storefront of the universe and fall into an endless void behind it. I was tempted even to try it, to walk around the cartoon of Niall's retreating back and find the nothing that lay beyond.

I stood and took a few steps and the earth pushed itself under my feet. But when Niall's back disappeared into the hotel door I didn't trust the ground to keep pace with me if I ran. I stood still and thought about what I should have done, what I should have said, my hand which never made it to his lips.

I pressed that hand against my own face but the salt air came between me and myself and I couldn't feel a thing.

SEVEN

Gillian

XIV

It's that dream, Mam. Even before she came back, it'd surprise me by returning when I thought I'd got rid of it for good. But now that she's here it's with me every night, and sometimes all day too. I hate her for that. I almost wish she'd go on and die. But I know if she does it'll only make things worse.

I don't know what time of the night it is. It's dark as fuck. I'm not all awake, but there are voices ... and she isn't in the bed any more. Her mother, in a pink dress, is taking her out the door by her arm. Gently, though: Clare isn't fighting. Nothing on but her little transparent nightgown.

I lie there for a minute, thinking how like Clare that is. And surely it's not my business. But I can tell. Before I even make the decision I'm up and sticking my feet in my shoes, spitting and cursing. The air outside the bed is cold.

(Teffie always laughs at what she calls my "intuitizing." She doesn't notice that I'm always right. Especially in my dreams. In my dreams I'm righter every time.)

All the way up and around, past the village, over to where the *Plassy* stands. Why it has to be all the way out here I couldn't tell you; there are hundreds of places you can go in the middle of the night to be alone. I'd know; I've been to most of them. I'm on my hands and knees, as there's nothing to hide behind, no trees or houses or telephone poles in this part of the world.

He's waiting, his face set in that creepy puss of his; I want to throw rocks at him but I don't want to be seen. I know I should stand up, I know what's coming and I know that if I just stand up so as he can see me it might make all the difference. But since that day at Teffie's place, when I threw the jar of pickled eggs at his head and he just about killed me, I've learned not to look him in the eye. My knees are bloody and my back hurts so I could hit any one of them, including Clare for being such a daft cunt as to do what Molly tells her.

Her mother hands her over like she's a Christmas basket. He throws her down on the rocks under him like she's made of rubber. I have to hide my eyes, but I can hear her shrieking right through his hand over her mouth, I can see him driving her right through the arm I've put over my face.

(I sometimes wonder what it was like for Teffie the first time. She grew to act like she liked it, but I wonder what she did the first time it happened. I wonder if she even remembers. That day I threw the jar at his head, though, she couldn't watch him do it to me. I've never figured out what that says about her.)

When he's done Clare lies limp as the dead, and he pulls himself up. He buttons and zips and turns his back; without a word to either of them he walks away. It's just a few steps before he vanishes into the night altogether, leaving behind a glowing swarm of sandflies which settle down onto the rocks.

I can't see Molly's face from this distance, just the smudge of her pink dress.

Clare's lying on the rocks with her nightgown all torn, and when she sees me her eyes go big as plums. Molly just looks at me. Her face takes my breath for a moment. Her eyes are huge stars, and her cloud of hair is all shimmering. Her mouth is a bit open as though she's after thinking of something she doesn't quite understand.

I say, "Aunt Molly, do you want to see something?"

Molly's face is twisting, twists more and more as I'm staring at her. It folds itself on top of itself like you used to fold the bread dough as you were kneading. Small sounds are coming from her face, little chirps and sobs and giggles and gurgles, as it folds itself into a mass of writhing face bits. Then it gives a small shriek and smooths itself out into a white blank mask, an empty page topped with a pile of gold hair.

I say, "Come on, then."

The *Plassy* is big as ten buildings, big as an ocean, snowing flakes of rust through the shadow I walk Molly and Clare into. I crawl inside, and it shrinks around me small like a glove. I want to tell Clare to wait on the beach, because it's dangerous in the boat, anything you touch can fall out from under you, but I don't want to break the spell Molly seems under.

I squirm up to the deck facing the ocean, and I hear the two of them crawl up behind me. We stand for a while against the railing, looking at the tide on its way in. I can see phosphorescence all through the water, as if someone's shaking the ocean like one of those gewgaws filled with liquid and glitter. We hang over the railing and I point with one hand out toward the horizon.

Molly strains forward, and the moon sticks to her hair. A mouth is forming itself in her empty face, smiling a bit.

I go blind. I grab her legs and roll her right over the railing, with a good firm push, to be sure she doesn't have a gentle fall. The howl her mouth lets loose rushes through me the way junk does; it lifts the rage right up and out of me; I look up and see it rising from me like steam. The sky goes clear and happy, and the stars dance above, and the ocean glitter dances below as she falls toward it, screaming.

Suddenly the earth pulls up toward us and it isn't that far

down any more. Her head, its face toward the ground, cracks itself against a rock, breaks in two and lies in halves; it looks like a split egg. One half, still stuck on her neck, is a mass of golden curls. The other lies face-up on the wet sand, a smooth white oval with a gaping, silent mouth. And then the tide rips in.

We're standing, Clare and me, craning our necks to look down as Molly lies there, her pink dress soaking to fuschia, her hair plastering and tangling with the waves. It seems a very long time. Minutes long.

Then Clare starts screaming. Her face stretches open the way plastic curls away from a cigarette burn. There's almost nothing left of her but the scream, and she turns it up to the sky.

I'm watching the waves as they push Molly and pull her and begin prying the clothes from her body. Clare isn't looking; her head is thrown back and she's screaming in a long hoarse wail. I watch as the ocean strips Molly's pink dress off and carries it away, leaving bare the white skin of her back and her little bum like a girl's. Then the waves begin to peel strips of flesh from her, thick clean strips that show the smooth bone beneath. Filet after filet curls in the salt and floats off, until she's nothing but ivory.

The phosphorescence washes over her and settles. She glitters like one of those nail files you used to have, Mam, the ones crusted with diamond dust. The undertow picks up her skeleton and carries it away from us until it's nothing but a rhinestone speck far out on the sea. Clare keeps on screeching, her half-blasted face to the sky.

I wrench myself awake and lie there wheezing and shaking, the pain of that rusted railing still pressed against my chest.

This is why I still keep the Bible right next to my bed, Mam. It used to be only for those rare wee-hour emergencies. But since Clare came back, I wake up with my lungs trying to kill me every night. Reaching out and putting my hand on the red cover brings the breath back. And it helps if the syringe is there, and something to put in it.

Small as Molly was, if you'd ever asked me if I'd be able to lift her all alone and throw her, all alone, over the side of a boat, so quick and easy that she never knew what hit her till she was dead, I would have said no. Not all by myself. When I told you, you said it must have been the rage made me so strong.

That night, once the *gardaí* had gone and you'd put us to bed in my yellow room ... I loved that yellow room, Mam ... only when the quiet came over us did I understand what'd happened.

We were lying in my bed side by side and I was listening to Clare's breath all watery and broken with hiccoughs. I thought suddenly of the night before, when we'd all been on the pier and I'd fallen drunk in the water. I couldn't remember a thing except the greasy cold feel of the ocean as it swallowed me, and then the painful grip of Teffie's hands under my arms. Lying in the dark next to Clare, only the memory of Teffie's hands was keeping me in the bed. Otherwise I'd have been down on the pier and dead in an instant.

Clare turned over to look at me, her dark hair all knots, her eyes blank and hollow. It stopped me for a second. I'd never thought her beautiful before.

I sat up and flicked on the lamp. I could feel her watching me while I picked up the Bible from the bedside table and opened it.

Cursed be the day wherein I was born: let not the day wherein my mother bare me be blessed.

Because he slew me not from the womb; or that my mother might have been my grave, and her womb to be always great with me.

Wherefore came I forth out of the womb to see labour and sorrow, that my days should be consumed with shame.

That's Jeremiah. Chapter Twenty. I marked it by folding the page; the crease is still there today. I looked straight at the wall in front of me, and then down at Clare where she lay. I said, "I don't think I can live with myself."

She blinked her big dead eyes. "We don't have to," she whispered.

I watched her face, trying to find something in it that meant something to me. But I was cold all over, until I felt the memory of Teffie's hands under my arms again, hoisting me out of the sea. Then I wanted to cry.

Clare was waiting. I wanted to give her something. No, that makes it sound like a lie. I meant it as I said it. I said, "Will you be coming back some day?"

And she said, "When?"

Teffie's hands tight and brutal, the fingers breakable as rust. *Five years*, I thought. I knew even then that love isn't likely to last that long.

When she turned over and seemed to fall asleep, I opened the Bible to another page.

And God sent an angel unto Jerusalem to destroy it: and as he was destroying, the Lord beheld, and he repented him of the evil, and said to the angel that destroyed, It is enough, stay now thine hand.

That's why He's God, Mam, and the rest of us are what we are.

EIGHT

Clare

XV

When I woke up this morning I lay on my mattress and listened. Gilly was alone in the kitchen; Teffia hasn't been here. Since that night. I listened to the Bible pages turning. Turning and turning as though she wasn't reading but searching for something she'd lost.

I rambled out in a rumpled shirt and shorts and put the kettle on. Outside were birds and sunshine, a pretty day. I stood in the open door for a while, but although the weed had long worn off, the world was still as flat and cartoonlike as a card. I smelled the warm salt air, watched the villagers wheel things and drive things and shout those Irish words for "good morning" to one another, but it could have been a television screen for all it meant to me.

I wanted her to speak first but she didn't, so finally I turned around and watched her flip pages. "I won't be back tomorrow," I said.

She didn't answer.

I sat down across from her at the table and watched. Flip. Flip. Flip. I imagined snatching the Bible from under her brown hands and slapping it over the gas flame of the stove.

"If you want to be a good Catholic girl," I said, "you might want to give up smack and cursing and sex with whores."

"Kiss my skinny arse."

Maybe it's not smack at all. Isn't it supposed bring calm and carelessness? Her downturned eyes could have set the Good Book ablaze. I waited for her to say more but she kept turning the pages metronomically.

"Gilly."

Her hand paused in the air. "What?" Nothing moved but her lips.

"You need to bring your mother home."

"Don't tell me what I need." Her eyes were still on the pages. Flip. Flip.

"Your mother needs it."

Her eyes closed and she pressed her teeth together. "You don't know anything about it. Go away."

"Yes, I'll go away."

"That's not what I'm saying." She finally looked up at me and her jaw pulled into a little sneer. "You don't mean it in any case."

"I'm done, Gilly. I'm sorry." I folded my hands on the table, the way my counsellor Mr. Pike does. I could feel why he does that. It pulled me into a circle, which is a strong and helpful shape.

"I don't believe it." She shook her head slowly and looked down again. Flip. Flip. Flip.

"I'll wait for you, but if you don't come, I won't be back."

She closed the Bible with a slam, kicked the chair out from under her, grabbed the kettle from the stovetop and hurled it at me. The lid flew off and struck me on the shoulder. Warm water splattered over the table, splashed me from face to waist. The kettle bounced off the wall behind me, hit the floor with a clang and spun in bewilderment before settling into the dark wet arc on the wood.

We were silent for a moment. She was still but quivering.

Every time Gilly had fought with Teffia, the two of them snarling Irish words I couldn't understand, Gilly's face looked just like that. And that day I got back to the B&B after she'd left me and Teffia alone out on the rocks; I walked into her yellow bedroom that evening to find her staring at me with that same expression.

It's not the look she had when Mumma fell from the *Plassy* though. That night Gilly's face was smooth and cool, as if she was risking nothing.

"I know what you did," she said. "The whores in hell will keep the two of you good company."

She stood for a moment with an accusing finger suspended in the air and seemed to want me to say something. She turned, gave the chair another vicious kick and a curse and tore out the door and ran down the road toward the graveyard.

The birds stopped singing for a long moment. Then they chimed up again, their morning celebration turned to gleeful gossip.

I watched the red cloth cover of *King James* as it lay helpless in what would have been my tea. The worn gold edges of the pages buckled.

Through the door the sky was a wash of blue on a stone wall.

XVI

I went to the hotel pub one last time tonight. The bodhran player came to put the bodhran in my hands but I pushed it away, shook my head too quickly; I should have said something but I didn't know what the something was. He shrugged and returned to his place a bit affronted but then began ratt-tattting away and the silver-toothed grin settled back on his face.

Teffia was not in a white dress this evening and her feet were not bare. She was wearing a thin frock printed with roses, with sleeves to her elbows and a waist pulled behind by corset-like strings. White socks and little black boots with Victorian-type buttons covered her ankles; she could have been on her way to a royal tea party if her hair hadn't been a party all its own, a party where someone had set fire to the house. I barely knew her when she clomped into the bar instead of wafting in like an ocean wind. Then she turned her crackling tea-brown eyes and smiled right through me.

I am such a fool.

She began with *"Women of Erin"* and once again I wondered: *Isn't there enough sadness here without filling the pubs with more?* The patrons sat silent but it felt like a pose, like standing for the national anthem. When was done everyone clapped politely and returned to their conversations.

She started another, a giddy one this time with a canter of bodhran and whistle. The tourists kept on chattering, but two of the middle-aged women at the bar went silent and looked at me sideways. One leaned in to the other and muttered something in Irish. They glanced in unison at Teffia and then at me, their mouths drawn closed.

Panic rose in my chest. I looked up at Niall, who was standing near to me, his hand pulling a pint and his glass-blue eyes frozen on the two women. As they looked around furtively at him his eyes stayed steady but his jaw shifted. His hand released the beer tap with a jerk. One of the women barked something sharp in Irish but he slowly shook his head and spat something in return. They both raised their eyebrows, huffed, and turned their backs.

He finally noticed that I was watching. He placed the pint in front of me and leaned over the bar, the tail of his platinum hair slapping my shoulder and then falling away.

"Molly na gCuach ní Chuilleanáin," he murmured, jerking his chin toward Teffia and her song. *"Molly of the Ringlets."*

Teffia's eyes were sly and narrow. If her hair were slightly more on the side of gold it might come close to reminding me of my mother's.

> *Is fada liom uaim í uaim í:*
> *Is fada liom uaim í ó d'imigh sí:*
> *Is fada liom thíos agus thuas í:*
> *Molly na gcuach Ní Chuilleannáin*

I started to cry.

Niall leaned his elbows on the bar. I felt a brief sigh against my face, heard him thinking *O for the love of Christ.* Then his hand fell over mine. No one else seemed to notice or care, and Padraic the fat freckled barman didn't interrupt, even though the pub crackled with Irish calls for service through Teffia's song. I thought my skin would shiver right up off my bones.

That night when Teffia and her father had danced and the rain had broken the door open and sluiced the floor ... I'd barely arrived then and I didn't know a thing, but I'd felt like I was surrounded by a glass bubble. And I couldn't tell if the bubble was protecting me from the disease that made these people clap and laugh as Teffia's father whirled her around the pub, or if it was just preventing me from ever touching anyone.

Sitting here at this bar I'd sometimes wanted to cry like I was crying now, all the muscles in my body in spasm, whimpering. But I'd never cried where they could see. Not even with Gilly. The night my mother died I'd screamed until no sound came out any more, but I didn't cry.

Niall's fingers were running firmly over the skin of my hand, one finger slipping between two of mine to touch the tender web there; a jolt shook me from my crotch to the nape of my neck. He touched his thumb under my eye to catch a tear. Through my sobs I thought: *Doesn't it matter to him who sees?*

Those nights in the pub he would stop bustling for a moment and stand on the other side of the bar nearer to me than to anyone else. If I left my hand lying on the bartop he'd reach through the glass bubble and press it, maybe thinking himself invincible. He'd stroke my fingers and turn my palm up to place a kiss into it.

And then he was afraid and let me go home.

When I caught my breath I said, quietly enough that I didn't think anyone would hear but jagged with the remains of tears, "If you'd promise to take care of me, I think I could stand it."

We looked at one another for a long moment. Two thin waves of hair had escaped the buckle at his nape and fell around his face like a smooth doorway; I could see as I couldn't see before threads of grey-white in the birch gold. All the lines and crevices around his eyes and cheekbones and lips were motionless.

"You can't be asking me for that," he said.

He pushed a pile of napkins toward me; I picked one up and mopped my face with it. "You're the only thing that's ever made any *sense*." I slapped my hand flat on the bar and laid my forehead on it.

"No man on earth has ever made sense, love." That almost made me laugh; I let out a little snort from my dripping nose, reached a blind hand for a napkin.

He didn't speak for a moment, a long enough moment that I lifted my head. He was gazing over me at Teffia, who kept singing and singing and singing as though she wanted to kill me. I turned and crumpled the napkin in my hand, ready to fire it straight into her kitten face. But then Niall spoke.

"If there's anyone who's ever made sense," he said, "it's your Aunt Rosary."

I turned slowly around and picked up another napkin. I blew my nose, blew it again, dropped the dirty napkins on the bar top, keeping my eyes on him the whole time. "Um ... what?"

"Ah, you heard me." He grinned, picked up a garbage pail and swept the napkins into it.

"My Aunt Rosary is in a mental hospital."

He dropped the pail and leaned on the bar again. "And it makes sense, if you consider it."

I would not consider it. *God damn you, god damn you all,*

why are you making this so hard?

"I can't do anything for her now," I said thickly. "She doesn't even care."

Niall sighed, picked up both my hands in his, squeezed them together and rubbed the fingers lightly. Then his gaze strayed past me and I followed it to where Grainne was coming in the door, smiling and raising a hand to someone who shouted at her from one of the window tables. Her thick sheet of hair was glossy tonight, maybe because there was no wind outside to stir it up, and her glasses were clean and shiny. She was wearing a long thin cream-coloured coat over her print dress and it made her look almost elegant. She didn't seem to notice her husband leaning over the bar holding the tourist girl's hands in his. She made her way to the front corner where someone was waving her over.

I started to cry again, my throat closing up. The two women near me glanced and looked away as though I were a car wreck and they were ashamed of being interested. Fat Padraic scowled down the bar at me. Teffia sang louder and belligerently.

"It's you who needs to care, Clare," Niall said absently, his eyes still on Grainne. "Caring's hard, but it helps, I find."

"How would you know?"

I pulled my hands from his and shoved my pint of Guinness over the bar where it crashed into a puddle of glass splinters at his feet.

The pub fell silent except for Teffia's voice shaking and sweet as the surface of tea in a storm.

Niall signaled to Padraic and pointed to the smashed glass and pool of stout. Then he stepped around the bar, took me by the arm with firm fingers and guided me toward the door.

As we passed the window tables I looked over at Grainne, who was staring patiently at some point just beyond and to the left of me.

Once outside I wrenched away from him. The sunset light was warm and peach-rose, heavy like the air in a fruit orchard although the only smells were of salt and the waft of beer coming from the pub. The whole island seemed eerily quiet as though everyone had gone somewhere else for the evening. Even the pub sounds were distant and muffled through the heavy door.

"Go on," he said. His face was flushed with the sunset. "Run away, then. That's all this is, isn't it? If you wanted to die, Clare, you'd be after doing it long ago."

He put his hands in his pockets and leaned back against the door frame. A hint of breeze picked up the ends of his hair and I thought of angels. But he was standing so close and I couldn't help but think that if I just did the right thing, said the right thing, touched him in just the right way, all that patient resolve would crumble.

"I'm working up the courage." I tried to stare him defiantly in the eyes but I wasn't able; the sear of his blue gaze was too strong.

"It's not courage I'd call it."

I tossed my head back to look at the turquoise and pink of the flat sky, letting the last of the tears run away down the edges of my face. "We made a promise," I said. "We set the date."

"And when is that date, Clare?"

I didn't answer him, turned away to look over the hill to where all roads led to somewhere near the sea.

"You want to tell me," he said quietly. "You want me to

come and try to stop you. And I will, if you tell me." I said nothing. "No one is holding you to any promise. Gillian has a life now. And so do you."

"A life?" I bent and picked a stone up from the step, hurled it toward the ocean. "I've got nothing. I've got nobody." I watched the stone dive and land in the short grass not fifteen feet from where I stood.

I waited for the baby to kick me. It was the kind of moment it would choose to do that. But it seemed to be sleeping, or indifferent. I put my hand over my belly to check for it but I was no longer sure what to expect from it. What if it's all a mistake? I wondered. What if there's no baby, just a phantom surge of hormones and too much beer settling around my middle? Would that change anything?

"Listen to me," Niall said. "I want you to listen."

I set my mouth, wiped my cheeks with the back of my hand. The lap of the sea was slow and gentle far away down the hill, the air warmish and still as though waiting for thunder.

"I'm listening," I said.

His hair so white-gold and soft under the mandarin of the sunset, the pink drifting clouds reflecting blood into his face. His eyes brilliant glass-sharp blue.

"I cannot give you what you want. What you say you want, what you think you want. I don't even know who you're thinking I am. But I can be a friend to you if it would help you."

That's what he said, Auntie. Through the pub door I heard Teffia singing *"My Match It is Made"*. The peach light was fading fast into cold salt dusk.

> I got up two hours before day
> And I got a letter from my true love

And I heard the blackbird and the linnet say
That my love has crossed the ocean

I turned and ran off down the hill and wished it were truly night so he could see the darkness swallow me.

As I ran I wondered whether I should have told him that tonight's the night. But he was wrong. I didn't really want him to know. I ran heavily and breathlessly; any minute now I would crash through the tissue-paper facade that looked like the world and would fall into the emptiness beyond it.

I turned onto the road toward Gilly's house and stopped so abruptly that my feet skidded out from under me and I fell into the dust and pebbles of the road, scraping my elbows.

Halfway between me and the green house was a tiny long-limbed woman with a pile of pale ringlets. She was walking away from me; I couldn't see her face. The light was close to marble-grey now, and in it her hair was dull. She wore a pink sleeveless shift and stepped almost weightlessly along the gravel.

I lay in the dust of the road and watched her as she turned at Gilly's step and went into the house.

The air pulsed around me thick and stinging. I waited for screams, for lightning, for the house to burst into blue flame, for me to wake up. I watched the light in the kitchen window, watched for a shadow to move across it, listened for women's thin voices.

I lay there waiting until someone came around the road behind me. I looked up with a pulse of hope, but it was just an old woman, returning home with a pile of books under her arm and a heavy sack bending her back. She nodded at me, her eyebrows surprised, and said some Irish words; not the words for good evening; maybe she was asking if I was hurt. I was embarrassed enough to get up out of the dust and shake myself off and walk slowly and blurrily down to the house and inside.

It was empty except for a pot of cooling hambone soup on the stove and a loaf of shop soda-bread on the table. The kitchen light was glowing as the sunset had, just moments before, the shadows rich and cheerful as chocolate. There was no movement and the inner air was solid and uninterrupted.

I stood in the doorway for a while and thought about bubbles and how some of them are warm and bright inside and keep things in and safe instead of holding them at bay. I wondered: *When I'm dead will I forget this room?* It seemed impossible, and sad. Sadder than anything.

I called out several different names but no one answered.

I sat down at the kitchen table and waited for the dark, which was a long time coming, or for someone, who never came. Gilly's Bible was still on the tabletop, buckled and seeping red into gold, surrounded by a faint water stain. As the island outside the window closed its eyes I folded my hands in front of me on the table. I watched the steam over the soup pot slow and fade and disappear.

XVII

I wish there was a place inside the boat where with one step you could enter the deepest part of the sea. You could crash through the rusted skin and plunge into the water without ever making a decision. But there isn't. The *Plassy* was tossed far up on the rocks and from it the sea looks like a memory. Except when the tide is high it's a dry boat.

I crawl up through the scraps, through the seachain. You wouldn't think I'd be afraid any more, afraid of rusty cuts, of floors that could send me down to lie dry and waiting in a heap of gashes and cracked bones. But dying alone in a dead boat after days of tetanus fever was not the plan. That was not the promise.

I reach the railing and stop for a short breath, a view of the black greedy water that leads to Ireland. I think: I'd rather do this on the other side of Inisheer where I could imagine being washed, not toward Galway, but toward home, if the sea agreed to take me and not toss me up on this island again. But it wasn't my decision.

My hair fills with salt and wind, tangles like a bag of pretzels. The stars are out. The moon too, a sliver of white skin like the hard worn edge of a bodhran. It's cold and dark and I think about how cold Ireland is all the time and how rarely it's dark. Then I think of how I've never seen Ireland in the winter and I wonder if it would be anything like Newfoundland. Anything like the beach on Cape Spear where I dropped gnat-sized orange shells in seawater to make them burst into red like sulfur into flame.

The baby punches, shaking me. I clench a hand over my belly like a claw. Is it possible for someone to rip out their own insides? Would the body and the mind ever allow that? *It's your fault,* I tell the baby silently.

I have a flash: of Mumma standing on the edge of that pier on Quidi Vidi, looking out over the black water with me in her arms. There are stories like this which she told me so many times that I started to remember them myself.

The first memory of my own was that man she called my father.

They don't think I remember, but the first event of my life is looking at them in the bed. And then all those days and nights in the dimness of that house with the doors closed. I remember the scarred and yellowing blue-and-white paper borders around the bottom of the living-room walls. I remember peeking out the curtains one afternoon when Mumma was busy somewhere else, looking at the soup of soft snow almost up to the windowsill and the black distant claws of leafless trees. But mostly I remember him so tall and me so small that he couldn't even see me and I saw him everywhere.

The innards of the boat creak and crumble.

I freeze, my hands tight on the rusted railing. Ghosts, I think, ghosts in pink dresses with sunburst ringlet hair. Returning. Doing the same thing over and over and expecting a different result. Her big eyes and her fragile bones made mighty with the invincibility of the undead, coming to tell me the will of God or maybe to introduce me to Him with a push.

Or maybe Niall guessed the date and is coming to throw me over his skinny shoulder and carry me off the way men do to women. I doubt he could lift me though. And where would he take me? What would he do with me once he got me there? Set me on my feet and give me little lectures on the importance of knowing one's place.

Or maybe it's you, Auntie, come back from the madhouse to be my hope once more.

She pulls up beside me. Her shorn hair shows her thin eyes wide and full of stars: sparks trapped in jars of oil. She leans on her elbows and I see a gash running up the twig of her forearm, sliding with grey-black blood in the dark. She's wearing tiny shorts which show the bottom edges of her bum; her brown skin is all gooseflesh.

Last time we were here the sheet of her whipping hair hid her face.

We lean against the railing together and look out over the sea. My limbs and ears are shooting with cold. Everything but her is flat as canvas and, I know, hollow behind. I reach a hand ahead of me to touch the surface of the world but it's an illusion; the world is still real, it's me who's not right. She's gazing out toward the dim black shadow of the horizon, the grey edge of her profile fine and slim as a line of calligraphy. The wind rises higher; the stars around us shiver and then hold firm. The sea spits salt up at the moon.

She says,

"Except the Lord build the house, they labour in vain that build it."

The stopper of a sob blocks my throat.

"It is vain for you to rise up early, to sit up late, to eat the bread of sorrows: for so he giveth his beloved sleep."

I close my eyes and grit my teeth. This is not the time, Gilly, I think, but I can't speak.

"Lo, children are an heritage of the Lord: and the fruit of

the womb is his reward. As arrows are in the hand of a mighty man; so are children of the youth."

For a moment I think I see the white fringe of the sun where Ireland should be, but then the sea is black again.

"Happy is the man that hath his quiver full of them: they shall not be ashamed, but they shall speak with the enemies in the gate."

Then she's silent.

"Did you memorize that for my benefit," I ask roughly, "or is your head full of scripture quotes for all occasions?"

Gilly sighs. "Psalm one hundred twenty-seven," she says. "A song of degrees."

"Okay."

We help ourselves to another pause full of salt wind.

I tip my head back. Something is moving across the sky, swallowing the stars one by one, then mouthful by mouthful. The underside of the hand of God, I think, and almost laugh at myself. Why is the sky filling up? Does death hollow you out or flood you with something new? I can't decide which I want more: to feel nothing and know nothing, or to feel and know something that is not this.

Those nights when we all hung about the castle and the pub and the pier and the graveyard, as if the whole island was our own now that people were in bed — once in a while during those nights I felt something that was not this. Once in a while I'd say something and everyone would laugh as if I wasn't a stranger and Niall would put his arms around me as if I was a part of him that had left and come back and that he was so happy to see again. Once — maybe just once — Gilly looked at me as if she was surprised.

That night after Teffia hung off the pier and pulled Gilly

out of the ocean, after Teffia had run crying into the night and Gilly had laughed herself silent, I took off my jacket and wrapped Gilly in it to soak up the dregs of the sea. I shivered in my yellow dress and she shivered in my coat and I kept my arms around her until she looked up at me with her face full of wonder. The others were gathered about us in a bewildered knot; cigarettes were lit and murmurs broke out. But she kept gazing up at me trembling and small and finally, not knowing what else to do, I said, "You're all right, Gilly."

Her eyes, black and thick, widened and then closed. Her tight mouth softened and fell limp. She sank into something like sleep and Niall and I picked her up and carried her back to the B&B where I took her inside and ran a hot bath for her while the rest of the house refused to awaken and the morning crept in far too fast. I sat next to the tub as she soaked there half-conscious and I watched the tremors that barrelled through her tiny body and I didn't cry, although I couldn't for the life of me tell you why not. I sat there with her and she didn't even know I was there. She didn't know anything, least of all about me.

The air clings moist and cold. The waves hiss and boil and the wind might be carrying the distant bare murmurs of almost-sleeping voices from the hotel, from the village, people going on and living into the night and speaking to one another about things that matter as they are being said.

"I'm sorry about Teffia," I say.

Her arm moves against mine as she shrugs. "It was to be expected."

"How did you know?"

Gilly gives a short brutal laugh. "She calls it 'intuitizing.'"

I wait for her to go on but she just stares at the sea. Her

mouth is thin and hard and the sparks in her eyes are burning motionless.

"You don't forgive me," I say finally.

"No." She shakes her head with a single tense flick. "I won't forgive you that. But there are many things I haven't forgiven her, either."

The stars are gone, the moon a grey shadow. I turn around and lean against the railing. I can't see past the mangled iron of the port side of the *Plassy* but I imagine the stretch of rocks beyond, the rocks that lead to more rocks, to walls of silent stones, to small rises and small falls and to rocks and rocks again, and then to more sea that looks as though it laps and rolls forever. But it doesn't. The ocean isn't endless and even between this world and my world it doesn't crash and break the whole way. There are times and places when it runs smooth as skin.

"I'll make you a deal," Gilly says.

I turn back toward Galway and hang my head and shoulders over the railing. A spatter — rain? or sea spit? — touches my neck like the finger of someone wanting my attention. I almost go over the side then, with or without her. No deals, I think. I will not negotiate with a God who is so amused.

Gilly lays a bird-boned hand on my arm.

"I will make you a new promise," she says.

I turn my head to look up at her.

Against the liquid of the speckled sky her eyes are rigid, frozen. Afraid to let herself out, I think. Afraid of what she is capable of. But it's one thing to be trapped in boiling oil and it's another to be suspended, waiting. Behind the clouds a weak attempt at lightning flutters; it's rain and not sea that's spitting on me. I look down at the water again and lift my feet from the deck, testing my weight against the reliability of the railing. A few flakes of rust scatter and ride away on the wind.

"You don't keep your promises, Gilly." I let my hands dangle toward the uplifted arms of the water.

"I will. I will keep it."

"I don't believe you."

"Listen to me, Clary Sage."

I hold myself still, my arms hanging.

"If you'll come down from here with me now, I'll go get my mother and I'll bring her home."

The wind bites at her tufts of hair. The wet on her cheeks might be tears; she's shaking. But it's likely to be cold and not grief. My hair flaps around between us, slapping the side of her face.

The sky strains and groans with thunder, rips open, and wails.

Her hand is still on my wrist. I watch the blood running from her forearm onto mine, the black of it thinning to grey. I'm wearing the t-shirt she gave me to sleep in, the one that pushes my breasts together and shows my baby like a fat tumor over the top of my jeans, and the black machine-knit Aran sweater I bought at the souvenir shop. It's all soaked through in less than a minute. I pull my arm from her hand and I push the sweater from my shoulders, shake it off and let it fall to the rust iron floor. The rain coats me like slop thrown from a bucket.

I suddenly think of my yellow dress, the butter-yellow dress Mumma bought for me long ago in Galway, and I wish I'd worn it, I wish I looked exactly as I did the first day Gilly ever saw me, so she would remember.

I lean over the railing as far as I can without letting my toes leave the deck. Below, the sea thrashes up through the rocks to get me, rabid with foam, close as the ends of my fingers, it seems. But as long as I watch — it seems like a long time — it never manages to kiss the side of the *Plassy*. Not quite.

My mother must have been the prettiest corpse in the history of the world. As she plummetted toward the water she looked like a feathery fishing fly, all pink and gold against the black sky. I wish it had been me Gilly had pushed over. We could have tied Mumma up and left her in the guts of the boat, gagged like a muzzled poodle, her piles of gold hair filling up with flakes of rust. We could have frightened her and then let her live.

It wasn't Mumma she wanted to kill at all, of course. I wonder how many nights Gilly hung over the railing of the *Plassy* all alone, her hair whipping full of salt and rust.

The wind stops short, paralyzed. The quilt of cloud hesitates and, as though remembering the stove has been left on at home in Scandinavia, tears off toward Galway and keeps going and going until the sky is thin and silver-grey with the light that someone once told me is not stars at all but the thousand-year-old memory of what the stars once were. The rain pulls up and evaporates.

The ocean seems to struggle, to hurl itself one last time toward the side of the boat below us, but it's no use; even the sea has its limitations. It collapses back toward the lights of Galway, then wrenches toward us as though afraid it will be lonely if it goes too far. Panic swells in me like flame; the tide is about to retreat. The baby kicks me again: *I'm still here.*

With a grunt I heave myself over, grinding the rust off the

railing to a sift of snow under my hands, and flip so that my face greets the sky.

The air is thick and cold and liquid and I think for a while that it will bear me away from Inisheer and bring me safely and gently back to land, but the wind can't decide on a direction: Ireland? America? Or someplace altogether new? I watch the memories of the stars for longer than possible, watch them as the wind tries to hold me up.

The moist hands of the storm pull away. I hover in the shock of silence, suspended, and then the crash of my back against the beach of stones shakes me like a house when the earth trembles.

I watch the stars some more as I think about pain. Think about how you don't always anticipate how much or how little there will be.

Above on the deck of the boat I can see a splinter lean toward me, a splinter with slender eyes full of the bodhran moon, and I think, slow and amused as the sea comes up gentler this time: *It's not very far from there to here. Not very far at all.*

NINE

Molly

XVIII

The only thing that ever made me question my faith was the fact that you were born a girl. But it didn't occur to me: Wasn't Mary conceived without sin herself? That's what the feast of the Immaculate Conception is all about; not the beginnings of the Saviour but the beginnings of His mother. I didn't think of that at the time.

I'm sorry, my honey. The Lord gives us what He gives us but it's up to us to understand his plan. I wasn't worthy. I hoped you would be.

I want you to understand that he was a good man. They were all good men. He was such a good dancer. He'd pick me up and whirl me around as if I was a little girl, with all my hair streaming out. A river of gold, he'd say sometimes, with his hands in my hair. The ways that he touched me were so beautiful.

Once he walked away from us over the grey rocks of Inisheer I saw I'd failed. I waited for someone to tell me what to do.

The only voice I heard was your cousin Gillian's.

ten

Clare

XIX

The pink-swathed body of my mother streams from the sky and crashes through me, dissolves to shivers in a wave that smothers us both, and is washed away in magenta and gold rivulets.

The cartoon canvas of the world trembles and buckles. Out by Galway the horizon retreats and the *Plassy* looming over me rushes closer. If I look straight up I think I can see the zenith running, escaping, stretching the universe like a rubber band. At the nadir is the back of my head, throbbing like the skin of a struck drum.

Gilly appears over me, a bent black twig against the stars. She reaches down to hook her hands under my arms and pull me toward the side of the *Plassy*. I give a little shriek as my ribs stab at me. Gilly stops, hesitates, then drops me and tears off across the rocks; I hear stones flying against stones under the pounding of her little feet.

The water claws up from my shoes to my face, washes the wind out of my hair. I breath in as much salt as I can but I'm too slow. *Come on,* I think. *You can't take her with you but throw me back.*

The sea splashes and teases and laughs uncontrollably as though I'm a very good joke. The waves shimmy up and shimmy away, leaving little almost invisible jellyfish clinging to me and sending their soft tingling stings through my clothes.

When the waves aren't in my ears I can hear the wind buffetting the *Plassy* as though trying to tip it over on top of me.

I stare up at the rotting iron side leaning away toward the beach and imagine it trying to heave itself over and crash down, imagine myself crushed into splinters as though I were made of dissolving iron myself.

Too late. I close my eyes.

I'm standing on a rock above a river holding a red King James Bible in one hand and a copper knotwork ring in the other. I look first at one and then at the other. The Bible is damp and warped, the gold on the edges of its pages smudged. The copper is darkening and greenish. I look out over the river; far in the distance — and the distance seems to wander farther and farther away — just above the surface of the water, is a cloud of red hair billowing, retreating. I look down at the Bible clutched in my right hand and the ring lying on the palm of my left. I try to raise my arms and hurl something but the only thing I can move is my head. I look up and watch that cloud of red hair as it floats further and further but doesn't disappear. The baby gives a smug, victorious knock.

"Yes," I say out loud. "I hear you."

Far away, I hear shouts and the scrape of feet on stones.

XX

Gilly ran to the hotel with black blood running from her forearm down all her clothes. Niall called to send a helicopter to Galway for the doctor. He left Padraic in charge of the bar and came tearing down to the edge of the water with Grainne and Gilly behind him carrying blankets and towels and a bottle of whiskey.

Niall and Grainne took my arms and legs and Gilly slid her hands under my back and head and they lifted me as gently as they could. I gave a shriek and bit almost clean through my lip. The back of my skull was ready to pound right through my forehead and I thought for a hysterical moment that every bone in my body was cracked. But as they lifted me out of the reaches of the ocean onto a dry blanket on the sand I realized that the only pain was spreading from my head and ribs, burning but diffused. I took a breath and closed my eyes against the tears which steamed up against the cold ocean wind.

Niall took a little Swiss army knife from his pocket and cut and peeled the clothes off me, tossed the soaked rags in a pile, plucked the jellyfish off my arms and legs and face. I felt almost shy at him seeing me naked after all these years; I wanted to make a joke but Grainne dropped a towel on me and began to rub me dry, as best she could without shifting me too much. Then they piled blankets on top of me.

Niall wanted to give me some whiskey but Grainne wouldn't let him lift my head. "Sure and we're after moving her now, what's the difference?" he asked but she was adamant.

She sat on the cold sand next to me, tugged my wet hair out from behind me and wrung it out like a long dishcloth. She laid another towel over my head and tucked it around without moving my neck. The stars and the moonfoam off the sea reflected in the thick smeared lenses of her glasses; her long hair glowed dully like the sand. She ran a hand over my forehead and said something quietly to Niall in Irish.

"Why don't you speak so she can understand," Niall said.

"You're cold, Clare," she said. "Are you hurting anywhere?"

Her voice was soft and clipped, a lot like yours, Auntie. A voice that only has time for the bare bones.

"Just my sides," I said, shivering, "and my head."

Gilly sat a couple of feet away, her black hair sticking up in all directions, her brown noodle arms wrapped around herself. She huddled with her knees up so I could see the undersides of her legs in their shorts all the way up to her crotch. She seemed to have blood all over her.

"Don't move," Grainne ordered. She stood and produced another blanket — "How many fucking blankets can three people carry?" I asked weakly but no one paid any attention to me — and wrapped it around Gilly's shoulders. Then she pulled Gilly's arm out and inspected the gash. She picked up a few pieces of my sliced-up T-shirt, trotted down to the surf and dipped them in, trotted back, sat down and dropped two of the rags in her lap. The third she wiped over Gilly's bloody forearm.

"That can't be too clean," Niall said.

"It's the best we've got at the moment." Grainne held out a thick hand for the whiskey bottle, which Niall handed to her. She poured whiskey on another rag and pressed that over the cut. Gilly pulled her breath in between her teeth. Grainne handed her the bottle and Gilly took a small sip while Grainne wrapped the third rag around the wound. There were bloodstains on Grainne's thin lumpish dress and spots of seawater spread over her pregnant belly but she didn't seem to notice that she was shivering herself. She sat down next to me and placed her hand on my hair, calming the shot of pain that was struggling through my head.

We heard the doctor, with voices around him, crunching over the stones from the direction of the landing pad. He appeared with a couple of the locals who Niall, I supposed, had sent down from the pub to meet his plane. They stood off to one side, looking bleary-eyed and not quite steady, while the doctor, a short wide-bellied man with a crown of bristly silver hair, settled down next to me. He had broken capillaries all across his big nose. The moon reflected off that shiny spider-veined nose until it was all I could see. I closed my eyes.

It turned out I'd cracked a few ribs and given myself a bit of a concussion. The jellyfish stings were no more serious than big mosquito bites. "It's a very lucky girl you are," said the doctor. "I don't think your lungs are punctured. And I think your baby will be fine." He looked at me sideways as though unsure whether that was what I'd wanted to hear. For a moment I wondered what baby he was talking about, so it punched me.

All *right,* I told it silently.

They lifted me onto the stretcher and the two half-drunk local men joggled me over the stones and out to the road where a van waited. I gritted my teeth against the stabs in my sides and watched the sky pass over me; the stars were dimming as the black of the night diluted to grey.

As they were loading me into the van head-first I lifted my head to look down toward my feet and see just Niall with the doctor and the men. "Gilly," I said to Niall.

"It's all right," he said, "Grainne's with her."

"What are they doing?" I tried to sit up but the man pulling the stretcher pushed me down again.

"She'll be all right, Clare." Niall hoisted himself up into the van next to me. "We're bringing you back to the house."

"Are you coming with me?"

"Yes, I'm coming with you." He settled into place and gazed absently out the rear doors of the van. One of the men slammed them closed.

"I'm not dead, am I, Niall?"

Niall started and stared at me. The moon through the window made his face as pale as shock. After a moment his shoulders relaxed. His mouth twitched into a smile and he gave a brief chuckle, touched my cheek with a long guinness hand. "I don't think so," he said indulgently. "You're cold as a spirit, but a bit heavier."

The motor choked and groaned and with a lurch we started along the road, each bounce and shudder piercing me. I closed my eyes and didn't make a single sound of pain.

When we reached Gilly's house the two locals hauled me and my stretcher out of the van. The doctor asked about putting me into a hot bath.

I thought suddenly of Gilly in that tub in the B&B that night so long ago, so long ago it seemed: Gilly lying curled and barely breathing, twitching and shivering and finally sinking into an insensible sleep as I sat, all wet with the cold sea and puckered with the hot steam, and wondered why I wasn't crying to wake the dead.

I told the doctor Gilly had only a shower, so he sent Niall for a hot water bottle and the men hauled me up the stairs to Gilly's bed. I thought of protesting that I slept downstairs but then her bed looked so inviting with its blue quilt that I said nothing. When they'd slid me into the blankets the doctor waved them out of the house. Niall tucked the hot water bottle into the thready bedclothes and smoothed the quilt around me and went downstairs to make tea.

The doctor, his nose glowing webby in the harsh bare light of the bulb overhead, spotted the syringe on top of the warped and still-damp Bible on the bedside table. *How odd,* I thought. With everything, Gilly had taken the time to come home and put the Good Book back where it belongs. The doctor frowned and picked the syringe up, pocketed it. "Take the Bible too," I said. He glanced in my direction, and then pretended he hadn't heard.

"I *am* dead," I muttered.

The doctor poked and prodded me some more. He pulled a sheath of bandages out of his bag and wrapped my torso up, turning and pushing me back and forth as if I were bread dough. I didn't much like him looking at my bare breasts; it reminded me of that ferry boat-hand again. I suddenly wondered where that boat-hand was right now, whether he was off procuring junk for Gilly or chatting up some girl in a Galway pub or here on Inisheer sound asleep beside some wide and familiar wife. I wondered if he had any memory of that little girl with the big boobs and her yellow dress; I wondered if he ever told that story to a bunch of his friends over the second or third pint. Surely he had.

The doctor trotted back down to the van and returned

with a cane. "You're not to be leaving this bed for a day or two except for the loo," he said. "After that, take it gently. I'll be at the hotel tonight. You oughtn't to sleep yet; wait until morning, and then have someone wake you every couple of hours. I'll tell Niall. Have them call me if there's anything." He turned away, not caring if I had any questions, and trundled away down the stairs.

I could hear Niall moving around below and the long building whine of the kettle, the moist exhalation of steam. The window was open, letting the night in to mingle with the cinnamon and sandalwood. I was cold. I watched the limp greyish curtains move with the light wind; the room began to swim a little and, knowing I shouldn't sleep but knowing I didn't care enough to stay awake, I thought mistily of calling for Niall.

I put a hand over my belly. *Still here,* the baby said almost imperceptibly.

I closed my eyes and nodded, sick and weak just above where the baby sat. "You win," I said.

I heard a scrabble outside the window.

Two long alabaster hands wrapped themselves around the sill. Teffia Mulvaney's eyes, sly and floating in a cloud of starlight-and-apple hair, inched up and hovered, fixed on me. She swung herself forward and somersaulted into the room, landed crouched on her haunches with a catlike thump, her rose-printed dress flying out and then settling around her and brushing the tops of her buttoned boots.

"It's yourself," she said, freckles squinting at me. She sank next to me on the braided rug, crosslegged.

"It's me."

"Are you all right?"

I hoped my smile was wry. "Depends what you mean."

Auntie, she's the most beautiful creature I've ever seen. Far more than Mumma although I never would have said that before. What does that mean? I can almost hear you ask. It seems like the sort of thing you would ask. Or maybe you'd say something like, Pretty is as pretty does. But maybe not. Surely you understand, Auntie. The line of thigh where she'd hitched up her dress; the perfect copper shadow through which the cream of her cheek peeked like a game. Her lips and their precise width. The tannin of her eyes. Everything about her trembles on the edge of too much, too full, too far. Trembles and balances.

That day I saw you and Teffia in the piano room, the smile just fading from your face, I could see it between you, within you, that hint of weakness. You understood Gilly. I understand Gilly too. There are certain people you just can't let go, and it's not because they make you happy.

With one slim hand she palmed the red Bible from the table onto her lap and flipped it open. "Where's Gilly?"

"I don't know."

"Well, I've come to see you, anyway." Her eyes were on the water-smudged pages: Ecclesiastes, I saw as if from across the world. "Padraic told me you're after falling off the boat."

"Yes."

"But you're not dead, I see."

"Well, if you say so."

She smiled and let the Bible rest on her lap, leaned back on her hands. Tossed the hair from her face so I could see every plush line.

"You'd have to be lucky," she said, "to die from falling off the *Plassy*. It's really not as far down as it might seem."

"You seem to know a lot about it."

She shrugged, still smiling, her eyes steady on me. Almost steady. Light from the bare bulb above us obscured the moonlight from the window, but I could see the sky behind her head turning from grey to dingy white.

If I'd known her better that night her father whirled her around the hotel pub I would have understood why no one looked away. On some people beauty is a crippling disease and to turn away from it would be unspeakably callous, like turning away from someone whose face is burned. They laughed and shouted and applauded for Teffia and her father the way they might have for a car crash victim dancing in his wheelchair.

"I need to know something," she said.

I swallowed. "All right."

Teffia's skin wavered between cream and pale ash in the bad light. Her eyes darted away from me. A long silence pressed the curtains back against the window. She jerked her head back to look at the ceiling and let her hair fall almost to the floor.

"Was it you who told her?"

I was weighted to the bed as if by stones dragging me to the bottom. She kept on staring at the ceiling as though it wasn't me she was asking at all, or as though she already knew the answer.

"Told who what?"

She lowered her chin and gave a little impatient sigh. I almost laughed. The baby kicked me sharply like a teacher slapping the shoulder of an insolent child.

"She said something about 'intuitizing,'" I said. I lifted an arm to scratch at a jellyfish sting across my cheek.

Teffia's lips twisted. "Ah." Her eyes were placid with disbelief. More than my ribs, the lazy angles of her legs and arms were hurting me. The Bible lay still on her lap; my eye fell on the words: *Is there any thing whereof it may be said, See, this is new?*

"What does it matter?" I spat. "You could fuck her mother and Gilly would still spread out like a kite for you."

The peach-pink of the flowers on her dress rose under her cheeks. We watched each other, immobile, like two cats; it struck me what a useless cat I was, bound in the bed by tensor bandages and shock, while her hair bristled and the edges of her teeth sharpened themselves against one another. Her eyes, slowly and shockingly, boiled like tea.

"I don't suppose you've ever loved anything," she said.

She waited for me to answer her, as if there were an answer.

For Christ's sake, what's all this? Didn't trying to die count for anything, for a minute or two of peace? I wanted to lift my arms, to shout something — something about how little she would ever know. But a wave of fatigue rose up over me; I tried to raise my head, but the room wavered around the edges, then spun and dimmed.

I was on the pier again, that second before Gilly screamed "Otters!" Teffia and Niall and the boys and I sitting with a joint and some drunken jokes, the moon reflecting all over us. Teffia looking at me with sly laughing eyes, maybe thinking that I was all right by her. Niall's arm tight around my shoulders. Even the ocean on almost all sides was, for the shortest moment I've ever known, one more thing to be happy about.

And then we all leapt to our feet and Gilly dropped out of sight.

When I opened my eyes Teffia was gone. The curtains were flapping a little and all the scent of other places had been washed away by the smell of cold clean salt stones.

Niall appeared in the doorway with two cups of tea which were barely steaming, as though he'd left them on the counter a little too long. His face was drawn and tired, his eyes a little pink and full around the edges. I wondered for a shocked moment if he'd been crying. He handed me the cup of tea and sat down on the floor beside the bed, closer to me than Teffia had been. He set his cup on the floor in front of him and leaned his head against the edge of the mattress, his back to me, the waves of his long platinum hair agitated and frizzy from all the running and wind. I watched the back of his head, the weariness of it, thought of all the reasons to reach a hand to his hair and all the reasons not to. And I thought: *I should say thank you.*

But when I finally spoke, finally said his name, there was no answer. I waited and was about to say it again but then, seeing the slow motion of the thin back under the cascade of his hair, I realized he'd fallen asleep. Beside me, close enough for me to touch, he'd fallen asleep.

I watched the steady gentle rise and fall of his back for a little while. Then I watched out the window, for hours it seemed, as the dawn turned to day and the island began stirring itself with those Irish words for good morning.

XXI

A few days later, the afternoon I was finally able to get out of bed, I hobbled up to the pub to find Niall behind the bar and the bodhran player alone on the musicians' benches, thudding quietly away as though his bodhran was a ventriloquist's doll with whom he was having a hushed and private chat.

I'd had a scrap with Gilly that morning. She'd finally come out and said it. "I don't owe you a thing," she barked. "You'd be dead as a flayed duck right now if it were up to you. It was God who saved you."

"Perhaps you owe God, then." She'd made us porridge for breakfast and it was dreadful, only half-warm by the time I got to it and full of dry lumps.

"I only said it to get you off that damned boat," she said, "and you didn't oblige. Not in the way you were expected to, in any case."

"I think we're even then," I said.

She put her cowlicked black head in her hands, the bones of her forearms fragile as straws. The gash seems to be festering but she assures me it's fine, bathes it with lavender oil in the mornings and nights. I stood up and turned my bowl upside down in the sink, leaving the porridge in a mess of paste. I picked up my cane and limped out of the house.

It was a warm day, not sunny but softly moist and bright grey through the clouds. All along the road to the hotel sheep were wandering, chewing on things and thinking. One of them lifted its head over the wall to look at me, its mouth working stupidly. I stopped and we watched one another for a while. I wondered if a sheep just chews when it chews and just walks when it walks, if anything interferes with a sheep's just keeping on. I pictured this sheep wandering down to the *Plassy* in the middle of the night and gazing at it, masticating solemnly, tortured by some terrible sheep-crime it had committed.

The baby snorted. My cane slipped out from under me and I fell with a thud against the stone wall, roaring with laughter and holding one of my tender sides.

The sheep watched me, bemused, until it grew bored and wandered away. I wiped my eyes and continued up the hill.

When I sat down at the bar Niall put down his cloth and came to lean on his elbows in front of me. "You're feeling better," he said.

"Yes." His hair was not tied up today but fell around his shoulders like one of those shimmering curtains that can take the place of a door.

"How's the baby?"

I pulled up my shirt to expose my belly. "Ask it," I said.

Niall reached over the bar. His big white hand was cold against my skin. "Hello, baby," he said softly. "How are you going?" He waited for a moment, smiled, his crooked teeth glinting. "I don't understand what it's trying to say." He pulled his hand away.

We were silent for a moment, my eyes on the shiny surface of the dark wood bar, he leaning on his elbows and, I could feel it, watching me. When I looked up he leaned in a little closer and said, "You're not going to be precipitating yourself off any more boats, are you, Clare?"

I shook my head.

"And why not?"

I looked down at my belly. It was still exposed, white and

round and not very pretty, like a loaf of bread risen but unbaked. I folded my hands over it.

While I was lying there waiting for you to come, with the sea pulling at me and jellyfish hanging off my ears, I was glad I was only hurt, and not dead.

"As I was lying there in the water," I said, "I was thinking about how I wished I was on the other side of Inisheer," I said. "The side that faces home."

Niall leaned back a little, pulled a stool underneath him and sat. "What for?" he asked.

I started to shrug but he was serious. I frowned. Surely I didn't have to explain this to him of all people. But he was waiting so I thought about it for a moment.

"I guess I wanted to imagine my home was watching and praying for me, instead of Galway just sitting there not knowing who I am."

His eyebrows arched. He paused, then leaned a thin cheek against a thin hand, contemplating me. The bodhran player thumped away.

Finally Niall said, "A home is just a pile of stones in the ocean, Clare. In a small place, it's easy to see where home ends and ocean begins, that's all. A pile of stones cannot pray."

I was surprised into silence. Then I chuckled lightly. "That's not like what you said the other day, Niall."

He smiled, his head still tilted against his hand. He is a beautiful man, Auntie, no matter what the different parts of him might say. "No, indeed," he said, "it is not. But neither is it contradictory."

He got to his feet. The bodhran fell silent. Niall picked up his rag and turned to move off down the bar, but then he turned back again. "And what's more," he said, "it wasn't

Galway watching you at all. The *Plassy* faces toward the south, toward Doolin. Those waves would have washed you to a place you've never been." He paused, jogging the rag up and down in his hand, his gaze directed over my shoulder toward where the bodhran player sat. Then he stilled his hand and smiled at me again. "Or else, more likely, they'd have left you right where you were."

And then he disappeared into the kitchen. I watched the place where he'd been. I wished I'd asked him to do something for me: make me a sandwich, pull me a pint. But I hadn't, and this seemed as good a time as any to leave him be.

I turned around to look at the bodhran player. He winked and grinned; the metal in his mouth glinted. He held the drum and the tipper out to me. I shook my head but he didn't withdraw them and finally I went and sat down on the bench next to him.

I took the bodhran in my hands and felt the skin of it with my palm. *This is what Gilly's skin feels like.* Teffia's skin is soft underneath like a crust of bread and Niall's is sharp and rigid with bones. But Gilly's skin is tight and empty like the new skin of an ancient drum.

I handed the bodhran back to him and he bowed his head, his black eyes peering up at me under sly thick brows. He thudded the tipper against the skin a few times as I stepped away from him toward the door. When I looked back over my shoulder he kissed the end of the tipper and waved it toward me and then went back to his thumping with his face turned toward the ceiling serene and uninterrupted. As though I'd never been there.

I went home. Back to Gilly's house I mean, the green house whose paint the wind from the sea is stripping away.

Down the path that leads all across the island from the bottom up to the top and back down again from one shore to the other. On this side I could see almost all the way to Galway. Is it really Galway? I wondered for a sharp second, halting. But yes, it was, this side faced Galway for sure, and I could see the *Aran Flyer* on its way in. I should have known the difference where the *Plassy* was concerned.

When I arrived the kitchen door was open. From the step I smelled something odd; for a moment I wondered if I'd come to the right house.

Niall's wife Grainne was in Gilly's kitchen. She was taking off a grey apron, an apron stained with grease and traces of flour which looked much like the one I saw you in the first day I ever came to this island. At the table Gilly sat a little sullen, her left forearm newly bandaged from wrist to elbow. In front of her was a plate of roasted chicken and a basket of steaming soda buns. She looked up at me as I came in and her face moved in more than one direction, then settled into no expression at all.

Grainne smiled at me, said a quick word in Irish (I think it was "good evening") and dropped the apron into the dust on the wood floor.

I sat across from Gilly; Grainne sat next to her. I reached for the basket and took a bun, broke it open releasing a breath of steam. Grainne watched me as I took a bite. It was a bit tough and a little more soda than bun, prickling. I chewed and swallowed and put the two halves of it on the table, carefully side by side.

"Help yourself to some chicken in the oven," Grainne said.

I nodded but I didn't move. Gilly was eating in small steady bites but soon she slowed and put her fork down, wiping a hand across her mouth and then across the leg of her shorts. Only half her chicken breast was eaten and she hadn't touched the potatoes or peas. I expected Grainne to look at her with concern, to coax her into taking a few more bites, to push the basket of buns toward her. But Grainne was still looking at me. Under the low-riding rims of her big glasses her smile was thin; under her dress her baby bulged, solid and patient.

"I'll be leaving soon," I said to Gilly.

Gilly looked up and nodded. There were touches of grease at the corners of her mouth. "When?" she asked before standing to put on the kettle.

"I don't know. I'll see. Soon."

Grainne was looking at the still-warm plate of chicken and didn't seem to hear us. I wished suddenly that she'd leave, leave us alone, at least until I'm gone. But half a breast of chicken is more solid food than I've ever seen Gilly eat at one time. And not even Teffia sits down in this kitchen and stays a while.

Gilly stood at the open door looking out. I could hear echoes of the village beyond her but all I could see was the shape of her back etching a blank in the pale afternoon light.

"We'll go to Galway first, if you like," she said.

What's more, the smell of food drives all those other smells away.

Grainne stood and moved over to Gilly, put a brisk arm around her shoulders and hugged her against the side of her growing belly. Gilly's back did not relent but neither did she pull away. Grainne said something Irish and turned to flash me a quick smile; I hardly saw it because her face was in shadow. Then she slipped out the door, turning in the direction of the hotel, leaving the grey apron to lie in the dust.

"Rude as whispering," I said. I reached for Gilly's plate and pulled it toward me, suddenly ravenous. "What did she say?"

Gilly's face was still to the outside. "She said I should let her know when my mother is home, so she can come by and help me out."

The chicken was too cooked, the peas too soft, but the gravy was smooth and rich with drippings. I stroked a piece of my soda bun through it and chewed. Gilly turned to face me, her shoulder against the splintering door frame.

She looked so small, so girl-like, the shadow of her body just a reed in the doorway, the world outside huge with the sound of the ocean. I was afraid suddenly to leave her and go home, and not afraid for myself for once. But then she came beside me and picked up her fork again. She sat and together, bite by silent bite, we polished off the plate of chicken, potatoes and peas and half the basket of buns. The air cooled, as did the food, and the sounds outside changed from day sounds — donkeys, cars, shop bustle, children's recitations in the yard outside the Irish school — to night sounds — televisions, the clink and sizzle of supper.

She made tea and we drank it on the doorstep, not talking much, just looking down over the dead people below us and out over the water, listening to boats and children on the beach and the beginning noises of fiddles and drums and laughter floating down from the hotel. And for the first time since I've been back, the first time since that night when Gilly and I did what we did — because she couldn't have done it alone, a little girl like her — I thought I saw the oil in her eyes thin from black to amber so the sparks could swim freely. But it could have been a trick of the light.

A Note on Sources

All Biblical quotations were taken from the Thomas Nelson, Inc. 1977 edition of the King James Version.

The Irish and English lyrics for the Irish folk songs *"Mo Ghille Mear"* on page 66, *"My Match It is Made"* on pages 113-114 and 178-179, and *"Molly na gCuach ní Chuilleanáin"* on page 173, were taken from the liner notes of the Dara Records album *éist: songs in their native language.*

The quote on page 89 is from the traditional English children's song *"The Grand Old Duke of York."*

The 1996 edition of *Ireland: A Lonely Planet Travel Survival Kit* was extremely helpful in providing geographical data for this project.